Leaves of Grass

The Original 1855 Edition

by Walt Whitman

Leaves of Grass
The Original 1855 Edition

by Walt Whitman

Green Tail Classics publish current edition in 2023 with unique illustrations by Sasha Binder.

Cover copyright @2023 by Green Tail Classics

Note:

All efforts have been made to preserve original spelling and punctuation of the original edition, which may include old-fashioned English spellings of words and archaic variants.

Contents

Leaves of Grass

Song of Myself

I celebrate myself, and sing myself,
And what I assume you shall assume,
For every atom belonging to me as good belongs to you.

I loafe and invite my soul,
I lean and loafe at my ease observing a spear of summer grass.

My tongue, every atom of my blood, form'd from this soil, this
    air,
Born here of parents born here from parents the same, and their
    parents the same,
I, now thirty-seven years old in perfect health begin,
Hoping to cease not till death.

Creeds and schools in abeyance,
Retiring back a while sufficed at what they are, but never
    forgotten,
I harbor for good or bad, I permit to speak at every hazard,
Nature without check with original energy.

Houses and rooms are full of perfumes, the shelves are crowded
    with perfumes,
I breathe the fragrance myself and know it and like it,
The distillation would intoxicate me also, but I shall not let it.

The atmosphere is not a perfume, it has no taste of the
    distillation, it is odorless,
It is for my mouth forever, I am in love with it,

I will go to the bank by the wood and become undisguised and
    naked,
I am mad for it to be in contact with me.

The smoke of my own breath,
Echoes, ripples, buzz'd whispers, love-root, silk-thread, crotch
    and vine,
My respiration and inspiration, the beating of my heart, the
    passing of blood and air through my lungs,
The sniff of green leaves and dry leaves, and of the shore and
    dark-color'd sea-rocks, and of hay in the barn,

The sound of the belch'd words of my voice loos'd to the eddies
    of the wind,
A few light kisses, a few embraces, a reaching around of arms,
The play of shine and shade on the trees as the supple boughs
    wag,
The delight alone or in the rush of the streets, or along the fields
    and hill-sides,
The feeling of health, the full-noon trill, the song of me rising
    from bed and meeting the sun.

Have you reckon'd a thousand acres much? have you reckon'd the
    earth much?
Have you practis'd so long to learn to read?
Have you felt so proud to get at the meaning of poems?

Stop this day and night with me and you shall possess the origin
    of all poems,
You shall possess the good of the earth and sun, (there are
    millions of suns left,)
You shall no longer take things at second or third hand, nor look
    through the eyes of the dead, nor feed on the spectres in
    books,
You shall not look through my eyes either, nor take things from
    me,

You shall listen to all sides and filter them from your self.

I have heard what the talkers were talking, the talk of the
    beginning and the end,
But I do not talk of the beginning or the end.

There was never any more inception than there is now,
Nor any more youth or age than there is now,
And will never be any more perfection than there is now,
Nor any more heaven or hell than there is now.

Urge and urge and urge,
Always the procreant urge of the world.

Out of the dimness opposite equals advance, always substance
    and increase, always sex,
Always a knit of identity, always distinction, always a breed of
    life.
To elaborate is no avail, learn'd and unlearn'd feel that it is so.

Sure as the most certain sure, plumb in the uprights, well
    entretied, braced in the beams,
Stout as a horse, affectionate, haughty, electrical,
I and this mystery here we stand.

Clear and sweet is my soul, and clear and sweet is all that is not
    my soul.

Lack one lacks both, and the unseen is proved by the seen,
Till that becomes unseen and receives proof in its turn.

Showing the best and dividing it from the worst age vexes age,
Knowing the perfect fitness and equanimity of things, while they
    discuss I am silent, and go bathe and admire myself.

Welcome is every organ and attribute of me, and of any man
    hearty and clean,
Not an inch nor a particle of an inch is vile, and none shall be
    less familiar than the rest.

I am satisfied—I see, dance, laugh, sing;
As the hugging and loving bed-fellow sleeps at my side through
    the night, and withdraws at the peep of the day with stealthy
    tread,
Leaving me baskets cover'd with white towels swelling the house
    with their plenty,
Shall I postpone my acceptation and realization and scream at
    my eyes,
That they turn from gazing after and down the road,
And forthwith cipher and show me to a cent,
Exactly the value of one and exactly the value of two, and which
    is ahead?

Trippers and askers surround me,
People I meet, the effect upon me of my early life or the ward and
    city I live in, or the nation,
The latest dates, discoveries, inventions, societies, authors old
    and new,
My dinner, dress, associates, looks, compliments, dues,
The real or fancied indifference of some man or woman I love,
The sickness of one of my folks or of myself, or ill-doing or loss
    or lack of money, or depressions or exaltations,
Battles, the horrors of fratricidal war, the fever of doubtful news,
    the fitful events;
These come to me days and nights and go from me again,
But they are not the Me myself.

Apart from the pulling and hauling stands what I am,
Stands amused, complacent, compassionating, idle, unitary,

Looks down, is erect, or bends an arm on an impalpable certain rest,
Looking with side-curved head curious what will come next,
Both in and out of the game and watching and wondering at it.

Backward I see in my own days where I sweated through fog with
    linguists and contenders,
I have no mockings or arguments, I witness and wait.

I believe in you my soul, the other I am must not abase itself to
    you,
And you must not be abased to the other.

Loafe with me on the grass, loose the stop from your throat,
Not words, not music or rhyme I want, not custom or lecture, not
    even the best,
Only the lull I like, the hum of your valved voice.

I mind how once we lay such a transparent summer morning,
How you settled your head athwart my hips and gently turn'd
    over upon me,
And parted the shirt from my bosom-bone, and plunged your
    tongue to my bare-stript heart,
And reach'd till you felt my beard, and reach'd till you held my
    feet.

Swiftly arose and spread around me the peace and knowledge
    that pass all the argument of the earth,
And I know that the hand of God is the promise of my own,
And I know that the spirit of God is the brother of my own,
And that all the men ever born are also my brothers, and the
    women my sisters and lovers,
And that a kelson of the creation is love,
And limitless are leaves stiff or drooping in the fields,
And brown ants in the little wells beneath them,

And mossy scabs of the worm fence, heap'd stones, elder, mullein
and poke-weed.

A child said What is the grass? fetching it to me with full hands;
How could I answer the child? I do not know what it is any more
than he.

I guess it must be the flag of my disposition, out of hopeful green
stuff woven.

Or I guess it is the handkerchief of the Lord,
A scented gift and remembrancer designedly dropt,
Bearing the owner's name someway in the corners, that we may
see and remark, and say Whose?

Or I guess the grass is itself a child, the produced babe of the
vegetation.

Or I guess it is a uniform hieroglyphic,
And it means, Sprouting alike in broad zones and narrow zones,
Growing among black folks as among white,
Kanuck, Tuckahoe, Congressman, Cuff, I give them the same, I
receive them the same.

And now it seems to me the beautiful uncut hair of graves.

Tenderly will I use you curling grass,
It may be you transpire from the breasts of young men,
It may be if I had known them I would have loved them,
It may be you are from old people, or from offspring taken soon
out of their mothers' laps,
And here you are the mothers' laps.

This grass is very dark to be from the white heads of old mothers,
Darker than the colorless beards of old men,

9

Dark to come from under the faint red roofs of mouths.

O I perceive after all so many uttering tongues,
And I perceive they do not come from the roofs of mouths for
nothing.

I wish I could translate the hints about the dead young men and
    women,
And the hints about old men and mothers, and the offspring
    taken soon out of their laps.

What do you think has become of the young and old men?
And what do you think has become of the women and children?

They are alive and well somewhere,
The smallest sprout shows there is really no death,
And if ever there was it led forward life, and does not wait at the
    end to arrest it,
And ceas'd the moment life appear'd.

All goes onward and outward, nothing collapses,
And to die is different from what any one supposed, and luckier.

Has any one supposed it lucky to be born?
I hasten to inform him or her it is just as lucky to die, and I know
    it.

I pass death with the dying and birth with the new-wash'd babe,
    and am not contain'd between my hat and boots,
And peruse manifold objects, no two alike and every one good,
The earth good and the stars good, and their adjuncts all good.

I am not an earth nor an adjunct of an earth,
I am the mate and companion of people, all just as immortal and
    fathomless as myself,

(They do not know how immortal, but I know.)

Every kind for itself and its own, for me mine male and female,
For me those that have been boys and that love women,
For me the man that is proud and feels how it stings to be
    slighted,
For me the sweet-heart and the old maid, for me mothers and the
    mothers of mothers,
For me lips that have smiled, eyes that have shed tears,
For me children and the begetters of children.

Undrape! you are not guilty to me, nor stale nor discarded,
I see through the broadcloth and gingham whether or no,
And am around, tenacious, acquisitive, tireless, and cannot be
    shaken away.

The little one sleeps in its cradle,
I lift the gauze and look a long time, and silently brush away flies
    with my hand.

The youngster and the red-faced girl turn aside up the bushy hill,
I peeringly view them from the top.

The suicide sprawls on the bloody floor of the bedroom,
I witness the corpse with its dabbled hair, I note where the pistol
    has fallen.

The blab of the pave, tires of carts, sluff of boot-soles, talk of
    the promenaders,
The heavy omnibus, the driver with his interrogating thumb, the
    clank of the shod horses on the granite floor,
The snow-sleighs, clinking, shouted jokes, pelts of snow-balls,
The hurrahs for popular favorites, the fury of rous'd mobs,
The flap of the curtain'd litter, a sick man inside borne to the
    hospital,

The meeting of enemies, the sudden oath, the blows and fall,
The excited crowd, the policeman with his star quickly working
    his passage to the centre of the crowd,
The impassive stones that receive and return so many echoes,
What groans of over-fed or half-starv'd who fall sunstruck or in
    fits,
What exclamations of women taken suddenly who hurry home
    and give birth to babes,
What living and buried speech is always vibrating here, what
    howls restrain'd by decorum,
Arrests of criminals, slights, adulterous offers made,
    acceptances, rejections with convex lips,
I mind them or the show or resonance of them—I come and I
    depart.

The big doors of the country barn stand open and ready,
The dried grass of the harvest-time loads the slow-drawn wagon,
The clear light plays on the brown gray and green intertinged,
The armfuls are pack'd to the sagging mow.

I am there, I help, I came stretch'd atop of the load,
I felt its soft jolts, one leg reclined on the other,
I jump from the cross-beams and seize the clover and timothy,
And roll head over heels and tangle my hair full of wisps.

Alone far in the wilds and mountains I hunt,
Wandering amazed at my own lightness and glee,
In the late afternoon choosing a safe spot to pass the night,
Kindling a fire and broiling the fresh-kill'd game,
Falling asleep on the gather'd leaves with my dog and gun by my
    side.

The Yankee clipper is under her sky-sails, she cuts the sparkle
    and scud,

My eyes settle the land, I bend at her prow or shout joyously from
    the deck.

The boatmen and clam-diggers arose early and stopt for me,
I tuck'd my trowser-ends in my boots and went and had a good
    time;
You should have been with us that day round the chowder-kettle.

I saw the marriage of the trapper in the open air in the far west,
    the bride was a red girl,
Her father and his friends sat near cross-legged and dumbly
    smoking, they had moccasins to their feet and large thick
    blankets hanging from their shoulders,
On a bank lounged the trapper, he was drest mostly in skins, his
    luxuriant beard and curls protected his neck, he held his bride
    by the hand,
She had long eyelashes, her head was bare, her coarse straight
    locks descended upon her voluptuous limbs and reach'd to
    her feet.

The runaway slave came to my house and stopt outside,
I heard his motions crackling the twigs of the woodpile,
Through the swung half-door of the kitchen I saw him limpsy and
    weak,
And went where he sat on a log and led him in and assured him,
And brought water and fill'd a tub for his sweated body and
    bruis'd feet,
And gave him a room that enter'd from my own, and gave him
    some coarse clean clothes,
And remember perfectly well his revolving eyes and his
    awkwardness,
And remember putting plasters on the galls of his neck and
    ankles;
He staid with me a week before he was recuperated and pass'd
    north,
I had him sit next me at table, my fire-lock lean'd in the corner.

Twenty-eight young men bathe by the shore,
Twenty-eight young men and all so friendly;
Twenty-eight years of womanly life and all so lonesome.

She owns the fine house by the rise of the bank,
She hides handsome and richly drest aft the blinds of the window.

Which of the young men does she like the best?
Ah the homeliest of them is beautiful to her.

Where are you off to, lady? for I see you,
You splash in the water there, yet stay stock still in your room.

Dancing and laughing along the beach came the twenty-ninth
    bather,
The rest did not see her, but she saw them and loved them.

The beards of the young men glisten'd with wet, it ran from their
    long hair,
Little streams pass'd all over their bodies.

An unseen hand also pass'd over their bodies,
It descended tremblingly from their temples and ribs.

The young men float on their backs, their white bellies bulge to
    the sun, they do not ask who seizes fast to them,
They do not know who puffs and declines with pendant and
    bending arch,
They do not think whom they souse with spray.

The butcher-boy puts off his killing-clothes, or sharpens his knife
    at the stall in the market,
I loiter enjoying his repartee and his shuffle and break-down.

Blacksmiths with grimed and hairy chests environ the anvil,
Each has his main-sledge, they are all out, there is a great heat in
the fire.

From the cinder-strew'd threshold I follow their movements,
The lithe sheer of their waists plays even with their massive arms,
Overhand the hammers swing, overhand so slow, overhand so
sure,
They do not hasten, each man hits in his place.

The negro holds firmly the reins of his four horses, the block
swags underneath on its tied-over chain,
The negro that drives the long dray of the stone-yard, steady and
tall he stands pois'd on one leg on the string-piece,
His blue shirt exposes his ample neck and breast and loosens over
his hip-band,
His glance is calm and commanding, he tosses the slouch of his
hat away from his forehead,
The sun falls on his crispy hair and mustache, falls on the black
of his polish'd and perfect limbs.

I behold the picturesque giant and love him, and I do not stop
there,
I go with the team also.

In me the caresser of life wherever moving, backward as well as
forward sluing,
To niches aside and junior bending, not a person or object
missing,
Absorbing all to myself and for this song.

Oxen that rattle the yoke and chain or halt in the leafy shade,
what is that you express in your eyes?
It seems to me more than all the print I have read in my life.

My tread scares the wood-drake and wood-duck on my distant
    and day-long ramble,
They rise together, they slowly circle around.

I believe in those wing'd purposes,
And acknowledge red, yellow, white, playing within me,
And consider green and violet and the tufted crown intentional,
And do not call the tortoise unworthy because she is not
    something else,
And the jay in the woods never studied the gamut, yet trills pretty
    well to me,
And the look of the bay mare shames silliness out of me.

The wild gander leads his flock through the cool night,
Ya-honk he says, and sounds it down to me like an invitation,
The pert may suppose it meaningless, but I listening close,
Find its purpose and place up there toward the wintry sky.

The sharp-hoof'd moose of the north, the cat on the house-sill,
    the chickadee, the prairie-dog,
The litter of the grunting sow as they tug at her teats,
The brood of the turkey-hen and she with her half-spread wings,
I see in them and myself the same old law.

The press of my foot to the earth springs a hundred affections,
They scorn the best I can do to relate them.

I am enamour'd of growing out-doors,
Of men that live among cattle or taste of the ocean or woods,
Of the builders and steerers of ships and the wielders of axes and
    mauls, and the drivers of horses,
I can eat and sleep with them week in and week out.

What is commonest, cheapest, nearest, easiest, is Me,

Me going in for my chances, spending for vast returns,
Adorning myself to bestow myself on the first that will take me,
Not asking the sky to come down to my good will,
Scattering it freely forever.

The pure contralto sings in the organ loft,
The carpenter dresses his plank, the tongue of his foreplane
    whistles its wild ascending lisp,
The married and unmarried children ride home to their
Thanksgiving dinner,
The pilot seizes the king-pin, he heaves down with a strong arm,
The mate stands braced in the whale-boat, lance and harpoon are
    ready,
The duck-shooter walks by silent and cautious stretches,
The deacons are ordain'd with cross'd hands at the altar,
The spinning-girl retreats and advances to the hum of the big
    wheel,
The farmer stops by the bars as he walks on a First-day loafe and
    looks at the oats and rye,
The lunatic is carried at last to the asylum a confirm'd case,
(He will never sleep any more as he did in the cot in his mother's
    bed-room;)
The jour printer with gray head and gaunt jaws works at his case,
He turns his quid of tobacco while his eyes blurr with the
    manuscript;
The malform'd limbs are tied to the surgeon's table,
What is removed drops horribly in a pail;
The quadroon girl is sold at the auction-stand, the drunkard nods
    by the bar-room stove,
The machinist rolls up his sleeves, the policeman travels his beat,
    the gate-keeper marks who pass,
The young fellow drives the express-wagon, (I love him, though I
    do not know him;)
The half-breed straps on his light boots to compete in the race,
The western turkey-shooting draws old and young, some lean on

their rifles, some sit on logs,
Out from the crowd steps the marksman, takes his position,
    levels his piece;
The groups of newly-come immigrants cover the wharf or levee,
As the woolly-pates hoe in the sugar-field, the overseer views
    them from his saddle,
The bugle calls in the ball-room, the gentlemen run for their
    partners, the dancers bow to each other,
The youth lies awake in the cedar-roof'd garret and harks to the
    musical rain,
The Wolverine sets traps on the creek that helps fill the Huron,
The squaw wrapt in her yellow-hemm'd cloth is offering
    moccasins and bead-bags for sale,
The connoisseur peers along the exhibition-gallery with half-shut
    eyes bent sideways,
As the deck-hands make fast the steamboat the plank is thrown
    for the shore-going passengers,
The young sister holds out the skein while the elder sister winds
    it off in a ball, and stops now and then for the knots,
The one-year wife is recovering and happy having a week ago
    borne her first child,
The clean-hair'd Yankee girl works with her sewing-machine or
    in the factory or mill,
The paving-man leans on his two-handed rammer, the reporter's
    lead flies swiftly over the note-book, the sign-painter is   with
    lettering blue and gold,
The canal boy trots on the tow-path, the book-keeper counts at
    his desk, the shoemaker waxes his thread,
The conductor beats time for the band and all the performers
    follow him,
The child is baptized, the convert is making his first professions,
The regatta is spread on the bay, the race is begun, (how the white
    sails sparkle!)
The drover watching his drove sings out to them that would stray,
The pedler sweats with his pack on his back, (the purchaser
    higgling about the odd cent;)

19

The bride unrumples her white dress, the minute-hand of the
    clock moves slowly,
The opium-eater reclines with rigid head and just-open'd lips,
The prostitute draggles her shawl, her bonnet bobs on her tipsy
    and pimpled neck,
The crowd laugh at her blackguard oaths, the men jeer and wink
    to each other,
(Miserable! I do not laugh at your oaths nor jeer you;)
The President holding a cabinet council is surrounded by the
    great Secretaries,
On the piazza walk three matrons stately and friendly with
    twined arms,
The crew of the fish-smack pack repeated layers of halibut in the
    hold,
The Missourian crosses the plains toting his wares and his cattle,
As the fare-collector goes through the train he gives notice by the
    jingling of loose change,
The floor-men are laying the floor, the tinners are tinning the
    roof, the masons are calling for mortar,
In single file each shouldering his hod pass onward the laborers;
Seasons pursuing each other the indescribable crowd is gather'd,
    it is the fourth of Seventh-month, (what salutes of cannon and
    small arms!)
Seasons pursuing each other the plougher ploughs, the mower
    mows, and the winter-grain falls in the ground;
Off on the lakes the pike-fisher watches and waits by the hole in
    the frozen surface,
The stumps stand thick round the clearing, the squatter strikes
    deep with his axe,
Flatboatmen make fast towards dusk near the cotton-wood or
    pecan-trees,
Coon-seekers go through the regions of the Red river or through
    those drain'd by the Tennessee, or through those of the
    Arkansas,
Torches shine in the dark that hangs on the Chattahooche or
Altamahaw,

Patriarchs sit at supper with sons and grandsons and great-
　　grandsons around them,
In walls of adobie, in canvas tents, rest hunters and trappers after
　　their day's sport,
The city sleeps and the country sleeps,
The living sleep for their time, the dead sleep for their time,
The old husband sleeps by his wife and the young husband sleeps
　　by his wife;
And these tend inward to me, and I tend outward to them,
And such as it is to be of these more or less I am,
And of these one and all I weave the song of myself.

I am of old and young, of the foolish as much as the wise,
Regardless of others, ever regardful of others,
Maternal as well as paternal, a child as well as a man,
Stuff'd with the stuff that is coarse and stuff'd with the stuff
　　that is fine,
One of the Nation of many nations, the smallest the same and the
　　largest the same,
A Southerner soon as a Northerner, a planter nonchalant and
　　hospitable down by the Oconee I live,
A Yankee bound my own way ready for trade, my joints the
　　limberest joints on earth and the sternest joints on earth,
A Kentuckian walking the vale of the Elkhorn in my deer-skin
　　leggings, a Louisianian or Georgian,
A boatman over lakes or bays or along coasts, a Hoosier, Badger,
　　Buckeye;
At home on Kanadian snow-shoes or up in the bush, or with
　　fishermen off Newfoundland,
At home in the fleet of ice-boats, sailing with the rest and tacking,
At home on the hills of Vermont or in the woods of Maine, or the
　　Texan ranch,
Comrade of Californians, comrade of free North-Westerners,
　　(loving their big proportions,)
Comrade of raftsmen and coalmen, comrade of all who shake

hands and welcome to drink and meat,
A learner with the simplest, a teacher of the thoughtfullest,
A novice beginning yet experient of myriads of seasons,
Of every hue and caste am I, of every rank and religion,
A farmer, mechanic, artist, gentleman, sailor, quaker,
Prisoner, fancy-man, rowdy, lawyer, physician, priest.

I resist any thing better than my own diversity,
Breathe the air but leave plenty after me,
And am not stuck up, and am in my place.

(The moth and the fish-eggs are in their place,
The bright suns I see and the dark suns I cannot see are in their
    place,
The palpable is in its place and the impalpable is in its place.)

These are really the thoughts of all men in all ages and lands, they
    are not original with me,
If they are not yours as much as mine they are nothing, or next to
    nothing,
If they are not the riddle and the untying of the riddle they are
    nothing,
If they are not just as close as they are distant they are nothing.

This is the grass that grows wherever the land is and the water is,
This the common air that bathes the globe.

With music strong I come, with my cornets and my drums,
I play not marches for accepted victors only, I play marches for
    conquer'd and slain persons.

Have you heard that it was good to gain the day?
I also say it is good to fall, battles are lost in the same spirit
    in which they are won.

I beat and pound for the dead,
I blow through my embouchures my loudest and gayest for them.

Vivas to those who have fail'd!
And to those whose war-vessels sank in the sea!
And to those themselves who sank in the sea!
And to all generals that lost engagements, and all overcome
    heroes!
And the numberless unknown heroes equal to the greatest heroes
    known!

This is the meal equally set, this the meat for natural hunger,
It is for the wicked just same as the righteous, I make
    appointments with all,
I will not have a single person slighted or left away,
The kept-woman, sponger, thief, are hereby invited,
The heavy-lipp'd slave is invited, the venerealee is invited;
There shall be no difference between them and the rest.

This is the press of a bashful hand, this the float and odor of hair,
This the touch of my lips to yours, this the murmur of yearning,
This the far-off depth and height reflecting my own face,
This the thoughtful merge of myself, and the outlet again.

Do you guess I have some intricate purpose?
Well I have, for the Fourth-month showers have, and the mica on
    the side of a rock has.

Do you take it I would astonish?
Does the daylight astonish? does the early redstart twittering
    through the woods?
Do I astonish more than they?

This hour I tell things in confidence,

I might not tell everybody, but I will tell you.

Who goes there? hankering, gross, mystical, nude;
How is it I extract strength from the beef I eat?

What is a man anyhow? what am I? what are you?

All I mark as my own you shall offset it with your own,
Else it were time lost listening to me.

I do not snivel that snivel the world over,
That months are vacuums and the ground but wallow and filth.

Whimpering and truckling fold with powders for invalids,
      conformity goes to the fourth-remov'd,
I wear my hat as I please indoors or out.

Why should I pray? why should I venerate and be ceremonious?

Having pried through the strata, analyzed to a hair, counsel'd
      with doctors and calculated close,
I find no sweeter fat than sticks to my own bones.

In all people I see myself, none more and not one a barley-corn
      less,
And the good or bad I say of myself I say of them.

I know I am solid and sound,
To me the converging objects of the universe perpetually flow,
All are written to me, and I must get what the writing means.

I know I am deathless,
I know this orbit of mine cannot be swept by a carpenter's
      compass,
I know I shall not pass like a child's carlacue cut with a burnt

24

stick at night.

I know I am august,
I do not trouble my spirit to vindicate itself or be understood,
I see that the elementary laws never apologize,
(I reckon I behave no prouder than the level I plant my house by,
    after all.)

I exist as I am, that is enough,
If no other in the world be aware I sit content,
And if each and all be aware I sit content.

One world is aware and by far the largest to me, and that is
    myself,
And whether I come to my own to-day or in ten thousand or ten
    million years,
I can cheerfully take it now, or with equal cheerfulness I can wait.

My foothold is tenon'd and mortis'd in granite,
I laugh at what you call dissolution,
And I know the amplitude of time.

I am the poet of the Body and I am the poet of the Soul,
The pleasures of heaven are with me and the pains of hell are with
    me,
The first I graft and increase upon myself, the latter I translate
    into new tongue.

I am the poet of the woman the same as the man,
And I say it is as great to be a woman as to be a man,
And I say there is nothing greater than the mother of men.

I chant the chant of dilation or pride,
We have had ducking and deprecating about enough,
I show that size is only development.

Have you outstript the rest? are you the President?
It is a trifle, they will more than arrive there every one, and
    still pass on.

I am he that walks with the tender and growing night,
I call to the earth and sea half-held by the night.

Press close bare-bosom'd night—press close magnetic nourishing
    night!
Night of south winds—night of the large few stars!
Still nodding night—mad naked summer night.

Smile O voluptuous cool-breath'd earth!
Earth of the slumbering and liquid trees!
Earth of departed sunset—earth of the mountains misty-topt!
Earth of the vitreous pour of the full moon just tinged with blue!
Earth of shine and dark mottling the tide of the river!
Earth of the limpid gray of clouds brighter and clearer for my
    sake!
Far-swooping elbow'd earth—rich apple-blossom'd earth!
Smile, for your lover comes.

Prodigal, you have given me love—therefore I to you give love!
O unspeakable passionate love.

Thruster holding me tight and that I hold tight!
We hurt each other as the bridegroom and the bride hurt each
    other.

You sea! I resign myself to you also—I guess what you mean,
I behold from the beach your crooked fingers,
I believe you refuse to go back without feeling of me,
We must have a turn together, I undress, hurry me out of sight of
    the land,

Cushion me soft, rock me in billowy drowse,
Dash me with amorous wet, I can repay you.

Sea of stretch'd ground-swells,
Sea breathing broad and convulsive breaths,
Sea of the brine of life and of unshovell'd yet always-ready graves,
Howler and scooper of storms, capricious and dainty sea,
I am integral with you, I too am of one phase and of all phases.

Partaker of influx and efflux I, extoller of hate and conciliation,
Extoller of amies and those that sleep in each others' arms.

I am he attesting sympathy,
(Shall I make my list of things in the house and skip the house
    that supports them?)

I am not the poet of goodness only, I do not decline to be the poet
    of wickedness also.

What blurt is this about virtue and about vice?
Evil propels me and reform of evil propels me, I stand indifferent,
My gait is no fault-finder's or rejecter's gait,
I moisten the roots of all that has grown.

Did you fear some scrofula out of the unflagging pregnancy?
Did you guess the celestial laws are yet to be work'd over and
rectified?

I find one side a balance and the antipedal side a balance,
Soft doctrine as steady help as stable doctrine,
Thoughts and deeds of the present our rouse and early start.

This minute that comes to me over the past decillions,
There is no better than it and now.

What behaved well in the past or behaves well to-day is not such

wonder,
The wonder is always and always how there can be a mean man
    or an infidel.

Endless unfolding of words of ages!
And mine a word of the modern, the word En-Masse.

A word of the faith that never balks,
Here or henceforward it is all the same to me, I accept Time
    absolutely.

It alone is without flaw, it alone rounds and completes all,
That mystic baffling wonder alone completes all.

I accept Reality and dare not question it,
Materialism first and last imbuing.

Hurrah for positive science! long live exact demonstration!
Fetch stonecrop mixt with cedar and branches of lilac,
This is the lexicographer, this the chemist, this made a grammar
    of the old cartouches,
These mariners put the ship through dangerous unknown seas.
This is the geologist, this works with the scalper, and this is a
    mathematician.

Gentlemen, to you the first honors always!
Your facts are useful, and yet they are not my dwelling,
I but enter by them to an area of my dwelling.

Less the reminders of properties told my words,
And more the reminders they of life untold, and of freedom and
    extrication,
And make short account of neuters and geldings, and favor men
    and women fully equipt,
And beat the gong of revolt, and stop with fugitives and them that

plot and conspire.

Walt Whitman, a kosmos, of Manhattan the son,
Turbulent, fleshy, sensual, eating, drinking and breeding,
No sentimentalist, no stander above men and women or apart
    from them,
No more modest than immodest.

Unscrew the locks from the doors!
Unscrew the doors themselves from their jambs!

Whoever degrades another degrades me,
And whatever is done or said returns at last to me.

Through me the afflatus surging and surging, through me the
    current and index.

I speak the pass-word primeval, I give the sign of democracy,
By God! I will accept nothing which all cannot have their
    counterpart of on the same terms.

Through me many long dumb voices,
Voices of the interminable generations of prisoners and slaves,
Voices of the diseas'd and despairing and of thieves and dwarfs,
Voices of cycles of preparation and accretion,
And of the threads that connect the stars, and of wombs and of
    the father-stuff,
And of the rights of them the others are down upon,
Of the deform'd, trivial, flat, foolish, despised,
Fog in the air, beetles rolling balls of dung.

Through me forbidden voices,
Voices of sexes and lusts, voices veil'd and I remove the veil,
Voices indecent by me clarified and transfigur'd.

I do not press my fingers across my mouth,
I keep as delicate around the bowels as around the head and
    heart,
Copulation is no more rank to me than death is.

I believe in the flesh and the appetites,
Seeing, hearing, feeling, are miracles, and each part and tag of me
    is a miracle.

Divine am I inside and out, and I make holy whatever I touch or
    am touch'd from,
The scent of these arm-pits aroma finer than prayer,
This head more than churches, bibles, and all the creeds.

If I worship one thing more than another it shall be the spread of
    my own body, or any part of it,
Translucent mould of me it shall be you!
Shaded ledges and rests it shall be you!
Firm masculine colter it shall be you!
Whatever goes to the tilth of me it shall be you!
You my rich blood! your milky stream pale strippings of my life!
Breast that presses against other breasts it shall be you!
My brain it shall be your occult convolutions!
Root of wash'd sweet-flag! timorous pond-snipe! nest of guarded
    duplicate eggs! it shall be you!
Mix'd tussled hay of head, beard, brawn, it shall be you!
Trickling sap of maple, fibre of manly wheat, it shall be you!
Sun so generous it shall be you!
Vapors lighting and shading my face it shall be you!
You sweaty brooks and dews it shall be you!
Winds whose soft-tickling genitals rub against me it shall be you!
Broad muscular fields, branches of live oak, loving lounger in my
    winding paths, it shall be you!
Hands I have taken, face I have kiss'd, mortal I have ever touch'd,
    it shall be you.

I dote on myself, there is that lot of me and all so luscious,
Each moment and whatever happens thrills me with joy,
I cannot tell how my ankles bend, nor whence the cause of my
    faintest wish,
Nor the cause of the friendship I emit, nor the cause of the
    friendship I take again.

That I walk up my stoop, I pause to consider if it really be,
A morning-glory at my window satisfies me more than the
    metaphysics of books.

To behold the day-break!
The little light fades the immense and diaphanous shadows,
The air tastes good to my palate.

Hefts of the moving world at innocent gambols silently rising
    freshly exuding,
Scooting obliquely high and low.

Something I cannot see puts upward libidinous prongs,
Seas of bright juice suffuse heaven.

The earth by the sky staid with, the daily close of their junction,
The heav'd challenge from the east that moment over my head,
The mocking taunt, See then whether you shall be master!

Dazzling and tremendous how quick the sun-rise would kill me,
If I could not now and always send sun-rise out of me.

We also ascend dazzling and tremendous as the sun,
We found our own O my soul in the calm and cool of the
    daybreak.

My voice goes after what my eyes cannot reach,
With the twirl of my tongue I encompass worlds and volumes of

worlds.

Speech is the twin of my vision, it is unequal to measure itself,
It provokes me forever, it says sarcastically,
Walt you contain enough, why don't you let it out then?

Come now I will not be tantalized, you conceive too much of
    articulation,
Do you not know O speech how the buds beneath you are folded?
Waiting in gloom, protected by frost,
The dirt receding before my prophetical screams,
I underlying causes to balance them at last,
My knowledge my live parts, it keeping tally with the meaning of
    all things,
Happiness, (which whoever hears me let him or her set out in
    search of this day.)

My final merit I refuse you, I refuse putting from me what I really
    am,
Encompass worlds, but never try to encompass me,
I crowd your sleekest and best by simply looking toward you.

Writing and talk do not prove me,
I carry the plenum of proof and every thing else in my face,
With the hush of my lips I wholly confound the skeptic.

Now I will do nothing but listen,
To accrue what I hear into this song, to let sounds contribute
    toward it.

I hear bravuras of birds, bustle of growing wheat, gossip of
    flames, clack of sticks cooking my meals,
I hear the sound I love, the sound of the human voice,
I hear all sounds running together, combined, fused or following,
Sounds of the city and sounds out of the city, sounds of the day

and night,
Talkative young ones to those that like them, the loud laugh of
    work-people at their meals,
The angry base of disjointed friendship, the faint tones of the
    sick,
The judge with hands tight to the desk, his pallid lips
    pronouncing a death-sentence,
The heave'e'yo of stevedores unlading ships by the wharves, the
    refrain of the anchor-lifters,
The ring of alarm-bells, the cry of fire, the whirr of swift-streaking
    engines and hose-carts with premonitory tinkles and color'd
    lights,
The steam-whistle, the solid roll of the train of approaching cars,
The slow march play'd at the head of the association marching
    two and two,
(They go to guard some corpse, the flag-tops are draped with
    black muslin.)

I hear the violoncello, ('tis the young man's heart's complaint,)
I hear the key'd cornet, it glides quickly in through my ears,
It shakes mad-sweet pangs through my belly and breast.

I hear the chorus, it is a grand opera,
Ah this indeed is music—this suits me.

A tenor large and fresh as the creation fills me,
The orbic flex of his mouth is pouring and filling me full.

I hear the train'd soprano (what work with hers is this?)
The orchestra whirls me wider than Uranus flies,
It wrenches such ardors from me I did not know I possess'd them,
It sails me, I dab with bare feet, they are lick'd by the indolent
    waves,
I am cut by bitter and angry hail, I lose my breath,
Steep'd amid honey'd morphine, my windpipe throttled in fakes
    of death,

At length let up again to feel the puzzle of puzzles,
And that we call Being.

To be in any form, what is that?
(Round and round we go, all of us, and ever come back thither,)
If nothing lay more develop'd the quahaug in its callous shell
    were enough.

Mine is no callous shell,
I have instant conductors all over me whether I pass or stop,
They seize every object and lead it harmlessly through me.

I merely stir, press, feel with my fingers, and am happy,
To touch my person to some one else's is about as much as I can
    stand.

Is this then a touch? quivering me to a new identity,
Flames and ether making a rush for my veins,
Treacherous tip of me reaching and crowding to help them,
My flesh and blood playing out lightning to strike what is hardly
    different from myself,
On all sides prurient provokers stiffening my limbs,
Straining the udder of my heart for its withheld drip,
Behaving licentious toward me, taking no denial,
Depriving me of my best as for a purpose,
Unbuttoning my clothes, holding me by the bare waist,
Deluding my confusion with the calm of the sunlight and pasture
    fields,
Immodestly sliding the fellow-senses away,
They bribed to swap off with touch and go and graze at the edges
    of me,
No consideration, no regard for my draining strength or my
    anger,
Fetching the rest of the herd around to enjoy them a while,

Then all uniting to stand on a headland and worry me.

The sentries desert every other part of me,
They have left me helpless to a red marauder,
They all come to the headland to witness and assist against me.

I am given up by traitors,
I talk wildly, I have lost my wits, I and nobody else am the
    greatest traitor,
I went myself first to the headland, my own hands carried me
    there.

You villain touch! what are you doing? my breath is tight in its
    throat,
Unclench your floodgates, you are too much for me.

Blind loving wrestling touch, sheath'd hooded sharp-tooth'd
    touch!
Did it make you ache so, leaving me?

Parting track'd by arriving, perpetual payment of perpetual loan,
Rich showering rain, and recompense richer afterward.

Sprouts take and accumulate, stand by the curb prolific and vital,
Landscapes projected masculine, full-sized and golden.

All truths wait in all things,
They neither hasten their own delivery nor resist it,
They do not need the obstetric forceps of the surgeon,
The insignificant is as big to me as any,
(What is less or more than a touch?)

Logic and sermons never convince,
The damp of the night drives deeper into my soul.

(Only what proves itself to every man and woman is so,
Only what nobody denies is so.)

A minute and a drop of me settle my brain,
I believe the soggy clods shall become lovers and lamps,
And a compend of compends is the meat of a man or woman,
And a summit and flower there is the feeling they have for each
    other,
And they are to branch boundlessly out of that lesson until it
    becomes omnific,
And until one and all shall delight us, and we them.

I believe a leaf of grass is no less than the journey work of the
    stars,
And the pismire is equally perfect, and a grain of sand, and the
    egg of the wren,
And the tree-toad is a chef-d'œuvre for the highest,
And the running blackberry would adorn the parlors of heaven,
And the narrowest hinge in my hand puts to scorn all machinery,
And the cow crunching with depress'd head surpasses any statue,
And a mouse is miracle enough to stagger sextillions of infidels.

I find I incorporate gneiss, coal, long-threaded moss, fruits,
    grains, esculent roots,
And am stucco'd with quadrupeds and birds all over,
And have distanced what is behind me for good reasons,
But call any thing back again when I desire it.

In vain the speeding or shyness,
In vain the plutonic rocks send their old heat against my
    approach,
In vain the mastodon retreats beneath its own powder'd bones,
In vain objects stand leagues off and assume manifold shapes,
In vain the ocean settling in hollows and the great monsters lying
    low,

In vain the buzzard houses herself with the sky,
In vain the snake slides through the creepers and logs,
In vain the elk takes to the inner passes of the woods,
In vain the razor-bill'd auk sails far north to Labrador,
I follow quickly, I ascend to the nest in the fissure of the cliff.

I think I could turn and live with animals, they are so placid and
    self-contain'd,
I stand and look at them long and long.

They do not sweat and whine about their condition,
They do not lie awake in the dark and weep for their sins,
They do not make me sick discussing their duty to God,
Not one is dissatisfied, not one is demented with the mania of
    owning things,
Not one kneels to another, nor to his kind that lived thousands of
    years ago,
Not one is respectable or unhappy over the whole earth.

So they show their relations to me and I accept them,
They bring me tokens of myself, they evince them plainly in their
    possession.

I wonder where they get those tokens,
Did I pass that way huge times ago and negligently drop them?

Myself moving forward then and now and forever,
Gathering and showing more always and with velocity,
Infinite and omnigenous, and the like of these among them,
Not too exclusive toward the reachers of my remembrancers,
Picking out here one that I love, and now go with him on
    brotherly terms.

A gigantic beauty of a stallion, fresh and responsive to my
    caresses,

Head high in the forehead, wide between the ears,
Limbs glossy and supple, tail dusting the ground,
Eyes full of sparkling wickedness, ears finely cut, flexibly moving.

His nostrils dilate as my heels embrace him,
His well-built limbs tremble with pleasure as we race around and
    return.

I but use you a minute, then I resign you, stallion,
Why do I need your paces when I myself out-gallop them?
Even as I stand or sit passing faster than you.

Space and Time! now I see it is true, what I guess'd at,
What I guess'd when I loaf'd on the grass,
What I guess'd while I lay alone in my bed,
And again as I walk'd the beach under the paling stars of the
    morning.

My ties and ballasts leave me, my elbows rest in sea-gaps,
I skirt sierras, my palms cover continents,
I am afoot with my vision.

By the city's quadrangular houses—in log huts, camping with
    lumber-men,
Along the ruts of the turnpike, along the dry gulch and rivulet
    bed,
Weeding my onion-patch or hosing rows of carrots and parsnips,
    crossing savannas, trailing in forests,
Prospecting, gold-digging, girdling the trees of a new purchase,
Scorch'd ankle-deep by the hot sand, hauling my boat down the
    shallow river,
Where the panther walks to and fro on a limb overhead, where
    the buck turns furiously at the hunter,
Where the rattlesnake suns his flabby length on a rock, where the
    otter is feeding on fish,

Where the alligator in his tough pimples sleeps by the bayou,

Where the black bear is searching for roots or honey, where the beaver pats the mud with his paddle-shaped tall;

Over the growing sugar, over the yellow-flower'd cotton plant, over the rice in its low moist field,

Over the sharp-peak'd farm house, with its scallop'd scum and slender shoots from the gutters,

Over the western persimmon, over the long-leav'd corn, over the delicate blue-flower flax,

Over the white and brown buckwheat, a hummer and buzzer there with the rest,

Over the dusky green of the rye as it ripples and shades in the breeze;

Scaling mountains, pulling myself cautiously up, holding on by low scragged limbs,

Walking the path worn in the grass and beat through the leaves of the brush,

Where the quail is whistling betwixt the woods and the wheat-lot,

Where the bat flies in the Seventh-month eve, where the great goldbug drops through the dark,

Where the brook puts out of the roots of the old tree and flows to the meadow,

Where cattle stand and shake away flies with the tremulous shuddering of their hides,

Where the cheese-cloth hangs in the kitchen, where andirons straddle the hearth-slab, where cobwebs fall in festoons from the rafters;

Where trip-hammers crash, where the press is whirling its cylinders,

Wherever the human heart beats with terrible throes under its ribs,

Where the pear-shaped balloon is floating aloft, (floating in it myself and looking composedly down,)

Where the life-car is drawn on the slip-noose, where the heat hatches pale-green eggs in the dented sand,

Where the she-whale swims with her calf and never forsakes it,

Where the steam-ship trails hind-ways its long pennant of
   smoke,
Where the fin of the shark cuts like a black chip out of the water,
Where the half-burn'd brig is riding on unknown currents,
Where shells grow to her slimy deck, where the dead are
   corrupting below;
Where the dense-starr'd flag is borne at the head of the
   regiments,
Approaching Manhattan up by the long-stretching island,
Under Niagara, the cataract falling like a veil over my
   countenance,
Upon a door-step, upon the horse-block of hard wood outside,
Upon the race-course, or enjoying picnics or jigs or a good game
   of base-ball,
At he-festivals, with blackguard gibes, ironical license,
   bull-dances, drinking, laughter,
At the cider-mill tasting the sweets of the brown mash, sucking
   the juice through a straw,
At apple-peelings wanting kisses for all the red fruit I find,
At musters, beach-parties, friendly bees, huskings, house
   raisings;
Where the mocking-bird sounds his delicious gurgles, cackles,
   screams, weeps,
Where the hay-rick stands in the barn-yard, where the dry-stalks
   are scatter'd, where the brood-cow waits in the hovel,
Where the bull advances to do his masculine work, where the
   stud to the mare, where the cock is treading the hen,
Where the heifers browse, where geese nip their food with short
   jerks,
Where sun-down shadows lengthen over the limitless and
   lonesome prairie,
Where herds of buffalo make a crawling spread of the square
   miles far and near,
Where the humming-bird shimmers, where the neck of the long-
   lived swan is curving and winding,
Where the laughing-gull scoots by the shore, where she laughs

41

her near-human laugh,
Where bee-hives range on a gray bench in the garden half hid by
    the high weeds,
Where band-neck'd partridges roost in a ring on the ground with
    their heads out,
Where burial coaches enter the arch'd gates of a cemetery,
Where winter wolves bark amid wastes of snow and icicled trees,
Where the yellow-crown'd heron comes to the edge of the marsh
    at night and feeds upon small crabs,
Where the splash of swimmers and divers cools the warm noon,
Where the katy-did works her chromatic reed on the walnut-tree
over
    the well,
Through patches of citrons and cucumbers with silver-wired
    leaves,
Through the salt-lick or orange glade, or under conical firs,
Through the gymnasium, through the curtain'd saloon, through
    the office or public hall;
Pleas'd with the native and pleas'd with the foreign, pleas'd with
    the new and old,
Pleas'd with the homely woman as well as the handsome,
Pleas'd with the quakeress as she puts off her bonnet and talks
    melodiously,
Pleas'd with the tune of the choir of the whitewash'd church,
Pleas'd with the earnest words of the sweating Methodist
    preacher, impress'd seriously at the camp-meeting;
Looking in at the shop-windows of Broadway the whole
    forenoon, flatting the flesh of my nose on the thick plate glass,
Wandering the same afternoon with my face turn'd up to the
    clouds, or down a lane or along the beach,
My right and left arms round the sides of two friends, and I in the
    middle;
Coming home with the silent and dark-cheek'd bush-boy,
    (behind me he rides at the drape of the day,)
Far from the settlements studying the print of animals' feet, or
    the moccasin print,

By the cot in the hospital reaching lemonade to a feverish patient,
Nigh the coffin'd corpse when all is still, examining with a candle;
Voyaging to every port to dicker and adventure,
Hurrying with the modern crowd as eager and fickle as any,
Hot toward one I hate, ready in my madness to knife him,
Solitary at midnight in my back yard, my thoughts gone from me
    a long while,
Walking the old hills of Judaea with the beautiful gentle God by
    my side,
Speeding through space, speeding through heaven and the stars,
Speeding amid the seven satellites and the broad ring, and the
    diameter of eighty thousand miles,
Speeding with tail'd meteors, throwing fire-balls like the rest,
Carrying the crescent child that carries its own full mother in its
    belly,
Storming, enjoying, planning, loving, cautioning,
Backing and filling, appearing and disappearing,
I tread day and night such roads.

I visit the orchards of spheres and look at the product,
And look at quintillions ripen'd and look at quintillions green.

I fly those flights of a fluid and swallowing soul,
My course runs below the soundings of plummets.

I help myself to material and immaterial,
No guard can shut me off, no law prevent me.

I anchor my ship for a little while only,
My messengers continually cruise away or bring their returns to
    me.

I go hunting polar furs and the seal, leaping chasms with a
    pike-pointed staff, clinging to topples of brittle and blue.

I ascend to the foretruck,

43

I take my place late at night in the crow's-nest,
We sail the arctic sea, it is plenty light enough,
Through the clear atmosphere I stretch around on the wonderful
    beauty,
The enormous masses of ice pass me and I pass them, the scenery
    is plain in all directions,
The white-topt mountains show in the distance, I fling out my
    fancies toward them,
We are approaching some great battle-field in which we are soon
    to be engaged,
We pass the colossal outposts of the encampment, we pass with
    still feet and caution,
Or we are entering by the suburbs some vast and ruin'd city,
The blocks and fallen architecture more than all the living cities
    of the globe.

I am a free companion, I bivouac by invading watchfires,
I turn the bridegroom out of bed and stay with the bride myself,
I tighten her all night to my thighs and lips.

My voice is the wife's voice, the screech by the rail of the stairs,
They fetch my man's body up dripping and drown'd.

I understand the large hearts of heroes,
The courage of present times and all times,
How the skipper saw the crowded and rudderless wreck of the
    steamship, and Death chasing it up and down the storm,
How he knuckled tight and gave not back an inch, and was
    faithful of days and faithful of nights,
And chalk'd in large letters on a board, Be of good cheer, we will
    not desert you;
How he follow'd with them and tack'd with them three days and
    would not give it up,
How he saved the drifting company at last,
How the lank loose-gown'd women look'd when boated from the
    side of their prepared graves,

How the silent old-faced infants and the lifted sick, and the
    sharp-lipp'd unshaved men;
All this I swallow, it tastes good, I like it well, it becomes mine,
I am the man, I suffer'd, I was there.

The disdain and calmness of martyrs,
The mother of old, condemn'd for a witch, burnt with dry wood,
    her children gazing on,
The hounded slave that flags in the race, leans by the fence,
    blowing, cover'd with sweat,
The twinges that sting like needles his legs and neck, the
    murderous buckshot and the bullets,
All these I feel or am.

I am the hounded slave, I wince at the bite of the dogs,
Hell and despair are upon me, crack and again crack the
    marksmen,
I clutch the rails of the fence, my gore dribs, thinn'd with the
    ooze of my skin,
I fall on the weeds and stones,
The riders spur their unwilling horses, haul close,
Taunt my dizzy ears and beat me violently over the head with
    whip-stocks.

Agonies are one of my changes of garments,
I do not ask the wounded person how he feels, I myself become
    the wounded person,
My hurts turn livid upon me as I lean on a cane and observe.

I am the mash'd fireman with breast-bone broken,
Tumbling walls buried me in their debris,
Heat and smoke I inspired, I heard the yelling shouts of my
    comrades,
I heard the distant click of their picks and shovels,
They have clear'd the beams away, they tenderly lift me forth.

I lie in the night air in my red shirt, the pervading hush is for my
    sake,
Painless after all I lie exhausted but not so unhappy,
White and beautiful are the faces around me, the heads are bared
    of their fire-caps,
The kneeling crowd fades with the light of the torches.

Distant and dead resuscitate,
They show as the dial or move as the hands of me, I am the clock
    myself.

I am an old artillerist, I tell of my fort's bombardment,
I am there again.

Again the long roll of the drummers,
Again the attacking cannon, mortars,
Again to my listening ears the cannon responsive.

I take part, I see and hear the whole,
The cries, curses, roar, the plaudits for well-aim'd shots,
The ambulanza slowly passing trailing its red drip,
Workmen searching after damages, making indispensable
    repairs,
The fall of grenades through the rent roof, the fan-shaped
    explosion,
The whizz of limbs, heads, stone, wood, iron, high in the air.

Again gurgles the mouth of my dying general, he furiously waves
    with his hand,
He gasps through the clot Mind not me—mind—the
    entrenchments.

Now I tell what I knew in Texas in my early youth,
(I tell not the fall of Alamo,
Not one escaped to tell the fall of Alamo,

The hundred and fifty are dumb yet at Alamo,)
'Tis the tale of the murder in cold blood of four hundred and
    twelve young men.

Retreating they had form'd in a hollow square with their baggage
    for breastworks,
Nine hundred lives out of the surrounding enemies, nine times
    their number, was the price they took in advance,
Their colonel was wounded and their ammunition gone,
They treated for an honorable capitulation, receiv'd writing and
    seal, gave up their arms and march'd back prisoners of war.

They were the glory of the race of rangers,
Matchless with horse, rifle, song, supper, courtship,
Large, turbulent, generous, handsome, proud, and affectionate,
Bearded, sunburnt, drest in the free costume of hunters,
Not a single one over thirty years of age.

The second First-day morning they were brought out in squads
    and massacred, it was beautiful early summer,
The work commenced about five o'clock and was over by eight.

None obey'd the command to kneel,
Some made a mad and helpless rush, some stood stark and
    straight,
A few fell at once, shot in the temple or heart, the living and dead
    lay together,
The maim'd and mangled dug in the dirt, the new-comers saw
    them there,
Some half-kill'd attempted to crawl away,
These were despatch'd with bayonets or batter'd with the blunts
    of muskets,
A youth not seventeen years old seiz'd his assassin till two more
    came to release him,
The three were all torn and cover'd with the boy's blood.

At eleven o'clock began the burning of the bodies;
That is the tale of the murder of the four hundred and twelve
    young men.

Would you hear of an old-time sea-fight?
Would you learn who won by the light of the moon and stars?
List to the yarn, as my grandmother's father the sailor told it to
    me.

Our foe was no skulk in his ship I tell you, (said he,)
His was the surly English pluck, and there is no tougher or truer,
    and never was, and never will be;
Along the lower'd eve he came horribly raking us.

We closed with him, the yards entangled, the cannon touch'd,
My captain lash'd fast with his own hands.

We had receiv'd some eighteen pound shots under the water,
On our lower-gun-deck two large pieces had burst at the first fire,
    killing all around and blowing up overhead.

Fighting at sun-down, fighting at dark,
Ten o'clock at night, the full moon well up, our leaks on the gain,
    and five feet of water reported,
The master-at-arms loosing the prisoners confined in the after-
    hold to give them a chance for themselves.

The transit to and from the magazine is now stopt by the
    sentinels,
They see so many strange faces they do not know whom to trust.

Our frigate takes fire,
The other asks if we demand quarter?
If our colors are struck and the fighting done?

Now I laugh content, for I hear the voice of my little captain,
We have not struck, he composedly cries, we have just begun our
    part of the fighting.

Only three guns are in use,
One is directed by the captain himself against the enemy's main
    mast,
Two well serv'd with grape and canister silence his musketry and
    clear his decks.

The tops alone second the fire of this little battery, especially
    the main-top,
They hold out bravely during the whole of the action.

Not a moment's cease,
The leaks gain fast on the pumps, the fire eats toward the powder
    magazine.

One of the pumps has been shot away, it is generally thought we
    are sinking.

Serene stands the little captain,
He is not hurried, his voice is neither high nor low,
His eyes give more light to us than our battle-lanterns.

Toward twelve there in the beams of the moon they surrender to
    us.

Stretch'd and still lies the midnight,
Two great hulls motionless on the breast of the darkness,
Our vessel riddled and slowly sinking, preparations to pass to the
    one we have conquer'd,
The captain on the quarter-deck coldly giving his orders through
    a countenance white as a sheet,
Near by the corpse of the child that serv'd in the cabin,

The dead face of an old salt with long white hair and carefully
    curl'd whiskers,
The flames spite of all that can be done flickering aloft and below,
The husky voices of the two or three officers yet fit for duty,
Formless stacks of bodies and bodies by themselves, dabs of flesh
    upon the masts and spars,
Cut of cordage, dangle of rigging, slight shock of the soothe of
    waves,
Black and impassive guns, litter of powder-parcels, strong scent,
A few large stars overhead, silent and mournful shining,
Delicate sniffs of sea-breeze, smells of sedgy grass and fields by
    the shore, death-messages given in charge to survivors,
The hiss of the surgeon's knife, the gnawing teeth of his saw,
Wheeze, cluck, swash of falling blood, short wild scream, and
    long, dull, tapering groan,
These so, these irretrievable.

You laggards there on guard! look to your arms!
In at the conquer'd doors they crowd! I am possess'd!
Embody all presences outlaw'd or suffering,
See myself in prison shaped like another man,
And feel the dull unintermitted pain.

For me the keepers of convicts shoulder their carbines and keep
    watch,
It is I let out in the morning and barr'd at night.

Not a mutineer walks handcuff'd to jail but I am handcuff'd to
    him and walk by his side,
(I am less the jolly one there, and more the silent one with sweat
    on my twitching lips.)

Not a youngster is taken for larceny but I go up too, and am tried
    and sentenced.

Not a cholera patient lies at the last gasp but I also lie at the last
    gasp,
My face is ash-color'd, my sinews gnarl, away from me people
    retreat.

Askers embody themselves in me and I am embodied in them,
I project my hat, sit shame-faced, and beg.

Enough! enough! enough!
Somehow I have been stunn'd. Stand back!
Give me a little time beyond my cuff'd head, slumbers, dreams,
    gaping,
I discover myself on the verge of a usual mistake.

That I could forget the mockers and insults!
That I could forget the trickling tears and the blows of the
    bludgeons and hammers!
That I could look with a separate look on my own crucifixion and
    bloody crowning.

I remember now,
I resume the overstaid fraction,
The grave of rock multiplies what has been confided to it, or to
    any graves,
Corpses rise, gashes heal, fastenings roll from me.

I troop forth replenish'd with supreme power, one of an average
    unending procession,
Inland and sea-coast we go, and pass all boundary lines,
Our swift ordinances on their way over the whole earth,
The blossoms we wear in our hats the growth of thousands of
    years.

Eleves, I salute you! come forward!
Continue your annotations, continue your questionings.

The friendly and flowing savage, who is he?
Is he waiting for civilization, or past it and mastering it?

Is he some Southwesterner rais'd out-doors? is he Kanadian?
Is he from the Mississippi country? Iowa, Oregon, California?
The mountains? prairie-life, bush-life? or sailor from the sea?

Wherever he goes men and women accept and desire him,
They desire he should like them, touch them, speak to them, stay
     with them.

Behavior lawless as snow-flakes, words simple as grass,
     uncomb'd head, laughter, and naivete,
Slow-stepping feet, common features, common modes and
     emanations,
They descend in new forms from the tips of his fingers,
They are wafted with the odor of his body or breath, they fly out
     of the glance of his eyes.

Flaunt of the sunshine I need not your bask—lie over!
You light surfaces only, I force surfaces and depths also.

Earth! you seem to look for something at my hands,
Say, old top-knot, what do you want?

Man or woman, I might tell how I like you, but cannot,
And might tell what it is in me and what it is in you, but cannot,
And might tell that pining I have, that pulse of my nights and
     days.

Behold, I do not give lectures or a little charity,
When I give I give myself.

You there, impotent, loose in the knees,
Open your scarf'd chops till I blow grit within you,

Spread your palms and lift the flaps of your pockets,
I am not to be denied, I compel, I have stores plenty and to spare,
And any thing I have I bestow.

I do not ask who you are, that is not important to me,
You can do nothing and be nothing but what I will infold you.

To cotton-field drudge or cleaner of privies I lean,
On his right cheek I put the family kiss,
And in my soul I swear I never will deny him.

On women fit for conception I start bigger and nimbler babes.
(This day I am jetting the stuff of far more arrogant republics.)

To any one dying, thither I speed and twist the knob of the door.
Turn the bed-clothes toward the foot of the bed,
Let the physician and the priest go home.

I seize the descending man and raise him with resistless will,
O despairer, here is my neck,
By God, you shall not go down! hang your whole weight upon me.

I dilate you with tremendous breath, I buoy you up,
Every room of the house do I fill with an arm'd force,
Lovers of me, bafflers of graves.

Sleep—I and they keep guard all night,
Not doubt, not decease shall dare to lay finger upon you,
I have embraced you, and henceforth possess you to myself,
And when you rise in the morning you will find what I tell you is
    so.

I am he bringing help for the sick as they pant on their backs,
And for strong upright men I bring yet more needed help.

I heard what was said of the universe,
Heard it and heard it of several thousand years;
It is middling well as far as it goes—but is that all?

Magnifying and applying come I,
Outbidding at the start the old cautious hucksters,
Taking myself the exact dimensions of Jehovah,
Lithographing Kronos, Zeus his son, and Hercules his grandson,
Buying drafts of Osiris, Isis, Belus, Brahma, Buddha,
In my portfolio placing Manito loose, Allah on a leaf, the crucifix
    engraved,
With Odin and the hideous-faced Mexitli and every idol and
    image,
Taking them all for what they are worth and not a cent more,
Admitting they were alive and did the work of their days,
(They bore mites as for unfledg'd birds who have now to rise and
    fly and sing for themselves,)
Accepting the rough deific sketches to fill out better in myself,
    bestowing them freely on each man and woman I see,
Discovering as much or more in a framer framing a house,
Putting higher claims for him there with his roll'd-up sleeves
    driving the mallet and chisel,
Not objecting to special revelations, considering a curl of smoke
    or a hair on the back of my hand just as curious as any
    revelation,
Lads ahold of fire-engines and hook-and-ladder ropes no less to
    me than the gods of the antique wars,
Minding their voices peal through the crash of destruction,
Their brawny limbs passing safe over charr'd laths, their white
    foreheads whole and unhurt out of the flames;
By the mechanic's wife with her babe at her nipple interceding
    for every person born,
Three scythes at harvest whizzing in a row from three lusty angels
    with shirts bagg'd out at their waists,
The snag-tooth'd hostler with red hair redeeming sins past and
    to come,

56

Selling all he possesses, traveling on foot to fee lawyers for his
    brother and sit by him while he is tried for forgery;
What was strewn in the amplest strewing the square rod about
    me, and not filling the square rod then,
The bull and the bug never worshipp'd half enough,
Dung and dirt more admirable than was dream'd,
The supernatural of no account, myself waiting my time to be one
    of the supremes,
The day getting ready for me when I shall do as much good as the
    best, and be as prodigious;
By my life-lumps! becoming already a creator,
Putting myself here and now to the ambush'd womb of the
    shadows.

A call in the midst of the crowd,
My own voice, orotund sweeping and final.

Come my children,
Come my boys and girls, my women, household and intimates,
Now the performer launches his nerve, he has pass'd his prelude
    on the reeds within.

Easily written loose-finger'd chords—I feel the thrum of your
    climax and close.

My head slues round on my neck,
Music rolls, but not from the organ,
Folks are around me, but they are no household of mine.

Ever the hard unsunk ground,
Ever the eaters and drinkers, ever the upward and downward
    sun, ever the air and the ceaseless tides,
Ever myself and my neighbors, refreshing, wicked, real,
Ever the old inexplicable query, ever that thorn'd thumb, that
    breath of itches and thirsts,

Ever the vexer's hoot! hoot! till we find where the sly one hides
    and bring him forth,
Ever love, ever the sobbing liquid of life,
Ever the bandage under the chin, ever the trestles of death.

Here and there with dimes on the eyes walking,
To feed the greed of the belly the brains liberally spooning,
Tickets buying, taking, selling, but in to the feast never once
    going,
Many sweating, ploughing, thrashing, and then the chaff for
    payment receiving,
A few idly owning, and they the wheat continually claiming.

This is the city and I am one of the citizens,
Whatever interests the rest interests me, politics, wars, markets,
    newspapers, schools,
The mayor and councils, banks, tariffs, steamships, factories,
    stocks, stores, real estate and personal estate.

The little plentiful manikins skipping around in collars and tail'd
    coats
I am aware who they are, (they are positively not worms or fleas,)
I acknowledge the duplicates of myself, the weakest and
    shallowest is deathless with me,
What I do and say the same waits for them,
Every thought that flounders in me the same flounders in them.

I know perfectly well my own egotism,
Know my omnivorous lines and must not write any less,
And would fetch you whoever you are flush with myself.

Not words of routine this song of mine,
But abruptly to question, to leap beyond yet nearer bring;
This printed and bound book—but the printer and the
    printing-office boy?
The well-taken photographs—but your wife or friend close and

solid in your arms?
The black ship mail'd with iron, her mighty guns in her turrets—
    but the pluck of the captain and engineers?
In the houses the dishes and fare and furniture—but the host and
    hostess, and the look out of their eyes?
The sky up there—yet here or next door, or across the way?
The saints and sages in history—but you yourself?
Sermons, creeds, theology—but the fathomless human brain,
And what is reason? and what is love? and what is life?

I do not despise you priests, all time, the world over,
My faith is the greatest of faiths and the least of faiths,
Enclosing worship ancient and modern and all between ancient
    and modern,
Believing I shall come again upon the earth after five thousand
    years,
Waiting responses from oracles, honoring the gods, saluting the
    sun,
Making a fetich of the first rock or stump, powowing with sticks
    in the circle of obis,
Helping the llama or brahmin as he trims the lamps of the idols,
Dancing yet through the streets in a phallic procession, rapt and
    austere in the woods a gymnosophist,
Drinking mead from the skull-cap, to Shastas and Vedas
    admirant, minding the Koran,
Walking the teokallis, spotted with gore from the stone and knife,
    beating the serpent-skin drum,
Accepting the Gospels, accepting him that was crucified, knowing
    assuredly that he is divine,
To the mass kneeling or the puritan's prayer rising, or sitting
    patiently in a pew,
Ranting and frothing in my insane crisis, or waiting dead-like till
    my spirit arouses me,
Looking forth on pavement and land, or outside of pavement and
    land,

Belonging to the winders of the circuit of circuits.

One of that centripetal and centrifugal gang I turn and talk like
      man leaving charges before a journey.

Down-hearted doubters dull and excluded,
Frivolous, sullen, moping, angry, affected, dishearten'd,
      atheistical,
I know every one of you, I know the sea of torment, doubt, despair
      and unbelief.

How the flukes splash!
How they contort rapid as lightning, with spasms and spouts of
      blood!

Be at peace bloody flukes of doubters and sullen mopers,
I take my place among you as much as among any,
The past is the push of you, me, all, precisely the same,
And what is yet untried and afterward is for you, me, all, precisely
      the same.

I do not know what is untried and afterward,
But I know it will in its turn prove sufficient, and cannot fail.

Each who passes is consider'd, each who stops is consider'd, not
      single one can it fall.

It cannot fall the young man who died and was buried,
Nor the young woman who died and was put by his side,
Nor the little child that peep'd in at the door, and then drew back
      and was never seen again,
Nor the old man who has lived without purpose, and feels it with
      bitterness worse than gall,
Nor him in the poor house tubercled by rum and the bad
      disorder,
Nor the numberless slaughter'd and wreck'd, nor the brutish

koboo call'd the ordure of humanity,
Nor the sacs merely floating with open mouths for food to slip in,
Nor any thing in the earth, or down in the oldest graves of the
    earth,
Nor any thing in the myriads of spheres, nor the myriads of
    myriads that inhabit them,
Nor the present, nor the least wisp that is known.

It is time to explain myself—let us stand up.

What is known I strip away,
I launch all men and women forward with me into the Unknown.

The clock indicates the moment—but what does eternity
    indicate?

We have thus far exhausted trillions of winters and summers,
There are trillions ahead, and trillions ahead of them.

Births have brought us richness and variety,
And other births will bring us richness and variety.

I do not call one greater and one smaller,
That which fills its period and place is equal to any.

Were mankind murderous or jealous upon you, my brother, my
    sister?
I am sorry for you, they are not murderous or jealous upon me,
All has been gentle with me, I keep no account with lamentation,
(What have I to do with lamentation?)

I am an acme of things accomplish'd, and I an encloser of things
    to be.

My feet strike an apex of the apices of the stairs,

On every step bunches of ages, and larger bunches between the
    steps,
All below duly travel'd, and still I mount and mount.

Rise after rise bow the phantoms behind me,
Afar down I see the huge first Nothing, I know I was even there,
I waited unseen and always, and slept through the lethargic mist,
And took my time, and took no hurt from the fetid carbon.

Long I was hugg'd close—long and long.

Immense have been the preparations for me,
Faithful and friendly the arms that have help'd me.

Cycles ferried my cradle, rowing and rowing like cheerful
    boatmen,
For room to me stars kept aside in their own rings,
They sent influences to look after what was to hold me.

Before I was born out of my mother generations guided me,
My embryo has never been torpid, nothing could overlay it.

For it the nebula cohered to an orb,
The long slow strata piled to rest it on,
Vast vegetables gave it sustenance,
Monstrous sauroids transported it in their mouths and deposited
    it with care.

All forces have been steadily employ'd to complete and delight
    me,
Now on this spot I stand with my robust soul.

O span of youth! ever-push'd elasticity!
O manhood, balanced, florid and full.

My lovers suffocate me,
Crowding my lips, thick in the pores of my skin,
Jostling me through streets and public halls, coming naked to me
    at night,
Crying by day, Ahoy! from the rocks of the river, swinging and
    chirping over my head,
Calling my name from flower-beds, vines, tangled underbrush,
Lighting on every moment of my life,
Bussing my body with soft balsamic busses,
Noiselessly passing handfuls out of their hearts and giving them
    to be mine.

Old age superbly rising! O welcome, ineffable grace of dying days!

Every condition promulges not only itself, it promulges what
    grows after and out of itself,
And the dark hush promulges as much as any.

I open my scuttle at night and see the far-sprinkled systems,
And all I see multiplied as high as I can cipher edge but the rim
    of the farther systems.

Wider and wider they spread, expanding, always expanding,
Outward and outward and forever outward.

My sun has his sun and round him obediently wheels,
He joins with his partners a group of superior circuit,
And greater sets follow, making specks of the greatest inside
    them.

There is no stoppage and never can be stoppage,
If I, you, and the worlds, and all beneath or upon their surfaces,
    were this moment reduced back to a pallid float, it would
    not avail the long run,
We should surely bring up again where we now stand,
And surely go as much farther, and then farther and farther.

A few quadrillions of eras, a few octillions of cubic leagues, do
    not hazard the span or make it impatient,
They are but parts, any thing is but a part.

See ever so far, there is limitless space outside of that,
Count ever so much, there is limitless time around that.

My rendezvous is appointed, it is certain,
The Lord will be there and wait till I come on perfect terms,
The great Camerado, the lover true for whom I pine will be there.

I know I have the best of time and space, and was never measured
    and never will be measured.

I tramp a perpetual journey, (come listen all!)
My signs are a rain-proof coat, good shoes, and a staff cut from
    the woods,
No friend of mine takes his ease in my chair,
I have no chair, no church, no philosophy,
I lead no man to a dinner-table, library, exchange,
But each man and each woman of you I lead upon a knoll,
My left hand hooking you round the waist,
My right hand pointing to landscapes of continents and the
    public road.

Not I, not any one else can travel that road for you,
You must travel it for yourself.

It is not far, it is within reach,
Perhaps you have been on it since you were born and did not
    know,
Perhaps it is everywhere on water and on land.

Shoulder your duds dear son, and I will mine, and let us hasten

forth,
Wonderful cities and free nations we shall fetch as we go.

If you tire, give me both burdens, and rest the chuff of your hand
    on my hip,
And in due time you shall repay the same service to me,
For after we start we never lie by again.

This day before dawn I ascended a hill and look'd at the crowded
    heaven,
And I said to my spirit When we become the enfolders of those
    orbs,and the pleasure and knowledge of every thing in them,
    shall we be fill'd and satisfied then?
And my spirit said No, we but level that lift to pass and continue
    beyond.

You are also asking me questions and I hear you,
I answer that I cannot answer, you must find out for yourself.

Sit a while dear son,
Here are biscuits to eat and here is milk to drink,
But as soon as you sleep and renew yourself in sweet clothes, I
    kiss you with a good-by kiss and open the gate for your egress
    hence.

Long enough have you dream'd contemptible dreams,
Now I wash the gum from your eyes,
You must habit yourself to the dazzle of the light and of every
    moment of your life.

Long have you timidly waded holding a plank by the shore,
Now I will you to be a bold swimmer,
To jump off in the midst of the sea, rise again, nod to me, shout,
    and laughingly dash with your hair.

65

I am the teacher of athletes,
He that by me spreads a wider breast than my own proves the
    width of my own,
He most honors my style who learns under it to destroy the
    teacher.

The boy I love, the same becomes a man not through derived
    power, but in his own right,
Wicked rather than virtuous out of conformity or fear,
Fond of his sweetheart, relishing well his steak,
Unrequited love or a slight cutting him worse than sharp steel
    cuts,
First-rate to ride, to fight, to hit the bull's eye, to sail a
    skiff, to sing a song or play on the banjo,
Preferring scars and the beard and faces pitted with small-pox
    over all latherers,
And those well-tann'd to those that keep out of the sun.

I teach straying from me, yet who can stray from me?
I follow you whoever you are from the present hour,
My words itch at your ears till you understand them.

I do not say these things for a dollar or to fill up the time while
    I wait for a boat,
(It is you talking just as much as myself, I act as the tongue of
    you,
Tied in your mouth, in mine it begins to be loosen'd.)

I swear I will never again mention love or death inside a house,
And I swear I will never translate myself at all, only to him or her
    who privately stays with me in the open air.

If you would understand me go to the heights or water-shore,
The nearest gnat is an explanation, and a drop or motion of waves
    key,
The maul, the oar, the hand-saw, second my words.

No shutter'd room or school can commune with me,
But roughs and little children better than they.

The young mechanic is closest to me, he knows me well,
The woodman that takes his axe and jug with him shall take me
    with him all day,
The farm-boy ploughing in the field feels good at the sound of my
    voice,
In vessels that sail my words sail, I go with fishermen and seamen
    and love them.

The soldier camp'd or upon the march is mine,
On the night ere the pending battle many seek me, and I do not
    fail them,
On that solemn night (it may be their last) those that know me
    seek me.
My face rubs to the hunter's face when he lies down alone in his
    blanket,
The driver thinking of me does not mind the jolt of his wagon,
The young mother and old mother comprehend me,
The girl and the wife rest the needle a moment and forget where
    they are,
They and all would resume what I have told them.

I have said that the soul is not more than the body,
And I have said that the body is not more than the soul,
And nothing, not God, is greater to one than one's self is,
And whoever walks a furlong without sympathy walks to his own
    funeral drest in his shroud,
And I or you pocketless of a dime may purchase the pick of the
    earth,
And to glance with an eye or show a bean in its pod confounds
    the learning of all times,
And there is no trade or employment but the young man

following it may become a hero,
And there is no object so soft but it makes a hub for the wheel'd
　　universe,
And I say to any man or woman, Let your soul stand cool and
　　composed before a million universes.

And I say to mankind, Be not curious about God,
For I who am curious about each am not curious about God,
(No array of terms can say how much I am at peace about God
　　and about death.)

I hear and behold God in every object, yet understand God not in
　　the least,
Nor do I understand who there can be more wonderful than
　　myself.

Why should I wish to see God better than this day?
I see something of God each hour of the twenty-four, and each
　　moment then,
In the faces of men and women I see God, and in my own face in
　　the glass,
I find letters from God dropt in the street, and every one is sign'd
　　by God's name,
And I leave them where they are, for I know that wheresoe'er I
　　go,
Others will punctually come for ever and ever.

And as to you Death, and you bitter hug of mortality, it is idle to
　　try to alarm me.

To his work without flinching the accoucheur comes,
I see the elder-hand pressing receiving supporting,
I recline by the sills of the exquisite flexible doors,
And mark the outlet, and mark the relief and escape.

And as to you Corpse I think you are good manure, but that does
    not offend me,
I smell the white roses sweet-scented and growing,
I reach to the leafy lips, I reach to the polish'd breasts of melons.

And as to you Life I reckon you are the leavings of many deaths,
(No doubt I have died myself ten thousand times before.)

I hear you whispering there O stars of heaven,
O suns—O grass of graves—O perpetual transfers and
    promotions,
If you do not say any thing how can I say any thing?

Of the turbid pool that lies in the autumn forest,
Of the moon that descends the steeps of the soughing twilight,
Toss, sparkles of day and dusk—toss on the black stems that
    decay in the muck,
Toss to the moaning gibberish of the dry limbs.

I ascend from the moon, I ascend from the night,
I perceive that the ghastly glimmer is noonday sunbeams
    reflected,
And debouch to the steady and central from the offspring great
    or small.

There is that in me—I do not know what it is—but I know it is in
    me.

Wrench'd and sweaty—calm and cool then my body becomes,
I sleep—I sleep long.

I do not know it—it is without name—it is a word unsaid,
It is not in any dictionary, utterance, symbol.

Something it swings on more than the earth I swing on,

To it the creation is the friend whose embracing awakes me.

Perhaps I might tell more. Outlines! I plead for my brothers and
sisters.

Do you see O my brothers and sisters?
It is not chaos or death—it is form, union, plan—it is eternal
life—it is Happiness.

The past and present wilt—I have fill'd them, emptied them.
And proceed to fill my next fold of the future.

Listener up there! what have you to confide to me?
Look in my face while I snuff the sidle of evening,
(Talk honestly, no one else hears you, and I stay only a minute
longer.)

Do I contradict myself?
Very well then I contradict myself,
(I am large, I contain multitudes.)

I concentrate toward them that are nigh, I wait on the door-slab.

Who has done his day's work? who will soonest be through with
his supper?
Who wishes to walk with me?

Will you speak before I am gone? will you prove already too late?

The spotted hawk swoops by and accuses me, he complains of my
gab and my loitering.

I too am not a bit tamed, I too am untranslatable,
I sound my barbaric yawp over the roofs of the world.

The last scud of day holds back for me,
It flings my likeness after the rest and true as any on the shadow'd
     wilds,
It coaxes me to the vapor and the dusk.

I depart as air, I shake my white locks at the runaway sun,
I effuse my flesh in eddies, and drift it in lacy jags.

I bequeath myself to the dirt to grow from the grass I love,
If you want me again look for me under your boot-soles.

You will hardly know who I am or what I mean,
But I shall be good health to you nevertheless,
And filter and fibre your blood.

Failing to fetch me at first keep encouraged,
Missing me one place search another,
I stop somewhere waiting for you.

A Song for Occupations

A song for occupations!
In the labor of engines and trades and the labor of fields I find
    the developments,
And find the eternal meanings.

Workmen and Workwomen!
Were all educations practical and ornamental well display'd out
    of me, what would it amount to?
Were I as the head teacher, charitable proprietor, wise
    statesman, what would it amount to?
Were I to you as the boss employing and paying you, would that
    satisfy you?

The learn'd, virtuous, benevolent, and the usual terms,
A man like me and never the usual terms.

Neither a servant nor a master I,
I take no sooner a large price than a small price, I will have my
    own whoever enjoys me,
I will be even with you and you shall be even with me.

If you stand at work in a shop I stand as nigh as the nighest in the
    same shop,
If you bestow gifts on your brother or dearest friend I demand as
    good as your brother or dearest friend,
If your lover, husband, wife, is welcome by day or night, I must
    be personally as welcome,
If you become degraded, criminal, ill, then I become so for your
    sake,
If you remember your foolish and outlaw'd deeds, do you think I
    cannot remember my own foolish and outlaw'd deeds?
If you carouse at the table I carouse at the opposite side of the

table,
If you meet some stranger in the streets and love him or her, why
    I often meet strangers in the street and love them.

Why what have you thought of yourself?
Is it you then that thought yourself less?
Is it you that thought the President greater than you?
Or the rich better off than you? or the educated wiser than you?

(Because you are greasy or pimpled, or were once drunk, or a
    thief,
Or that you are diseas'd, or rheumatic, or a prostitute,
Or from frivolity or impotence, or that you are no scholar and
    never saw your name in print,
Do you give in that you are any less immortal?)

Souls of men and women! it is not you I call unseen, unheard,
    untouchable and untouching,
It is not you I go argue pro and con about, and to settle whether
    you are alive or no,
I own publicly who you are, if nobody else owns.

Grown, half-grown and babe, of this country and every country,
    in-doors and out-doors, one just as much as the other, I see,
And all else behind or through them.

The wife, and she is not one jot less than the husband,
The daughter, and she is just as good as the son,
The mother, and she is every bit as much as the father.

Offspring of ignorant and poor, boys apprenticed to trades,
Young fellows working on farms and old fellows working on
    farms,
Sailor-men, merchant-men, coasters, immigrants,
All these I see, but nigher and farther the same I see,

None shall escape me and none shall wish to escape me.

I bring what you much need yet always have,
Not money, amours, dress, eating, erudition, but as good,
I send no agent or medium, offer no representative of value, but
    offer the value itself.

There is something that comes to one now and perpetually,
It is not what is printed, preach'd, discussed, it eludes discussion
    and print,
It is not to be put in a book, it is not in this book,
It is for you whoever you are, it is no farther from you than your
    hearing and sight are from you,
It is hinted by nearest, commonest, readiest, it is ever provoked
    by them.

You may read in many languages, yet read nothing about it,
You may read the President's message and read nothing about it
    there,
Nothing in the reports from the State department or Treasury
    department, or in the daily papers or weekly papers,
Or in the census or revenue returns, prices current, or any
    accounts of stock.

The sun and stars that float in the open air,
The apple-shaped earth and we upon it, surely the drift of them
    is something grand,
I do not know what it is except that it is grand, and that it is
    happiness,
And that the enclosing purport of us here is not a speculation or
    bon-mot or reconnoissance,
And that it is not something which by luck may turn out well for
    us, and without luck must be a failure for us,
And not something which may yet be retracted in a certain
    contingency.

The light and shade, the curious sense of body and identity, the
    greed that with perfect complaisance devours all things,
The endless pride and outstretching of man, unspeakable joys
    and sorrows,
The wonder every one sees in every one else he sees, and the
    wonders that fill each minute of time forever,
What have you reckon'd them for, camerado?
Have you reckon'd them for your trade or farm-work? or for the
    profits of your store?
Or to achieve yourself a position? or to fill a gentleman's leisure,
    or a lady's leisure?

Have you reckon'd that the landscape took substance and form
    that it might be painted in a picture?
Or men and women that they might be written of, and songs
    sung?
Or the attraction of gravity, and the great laws and harmonious
    combinations and the fluids of the air, as subjects for the
    savans?
Or the brown land and the blue sea for maps and charts?
Or the stars to be put in constellations and named fancy names?
Or that the growth of seeds is for agricultural tables, or
    agriculture itself?

Old institutions, these arts, libraries, legends, collections, and
    the practice handed along in manufactures, will we rate them
    so high?
Will we rate our cash and business high? I have no objection,
I rate them as high as the highest—then a child born of a woman
    and man I rate beyond all rate.

We thought our Union grand, and our Constitution grand,
I do not say they are not grand and good, for they are,
I am this day just as much in love with them as you,
Then I am in love with You, and with all my fellows upon the

76

earth.

We consider bibles and religions divine—I do not say they are not
    divine,
I say they have all grown out of you, and may grow out of you still,
It is not they who give the life, it is you who give the life,
Leaves are not more shed from the trees, or trees from the earth,
    than they are shed out of you.

The sum of all known reverence I add up in you whoever you are,
The President is there in the White House for you, it is not you
    who are here for him,
The Secretaries act in their bureaus for you, not you here for
    them,
The Congress convenes every Twelfth-month for you,
Laws, courts, the forming of States, the charters of cities, the
    going and coming of commerce and malls, are all for you.

List close my scholars dear,
Doctrines, politics and civilization exurge from you,
Sculpture and monuments and any thing inscribed anywhere are
    tallied in you,
The gist of histories and statistics as far back as the records
    reach is in you this hour, and myths and tales the same,
If you were not breathing and walking here, where would they all
    be?
The most renown'd poems would be ashes, orations and plays
    would be vacuums.

All architecture is what you do to it when you look upon it,
(Did you think it was in the white or gray stone? or the lines of
    the arches and cornices?)

All music is what awakes from you when you are reminded by the
    instruments,

It is not the violins and the cornets, it is not the oboe nor the
    beating drums, nor the score of the baritone singer singing his
    sweet romanza, nor that of the men's chorus, nor that of the
    women's chorus,
It is nearer and farther than they.

Will the whole come back then?
Can each see signs of the best by a look in the looking-glass? is
    there nothing greater or more?
Does all sit there with you, with the mystic unseen soul?

Strange and hard that paradox true I give,
Objects gross and the unseen soul are one.

House-building, measuring, sawing the boards,
Blacksmithing, glass-blowing, nail-making, coopering, tin-
    roofing, shingle-dressing,
Ship-joining, dock-building, fish-curing, flagging of sidewalks by
    flaggers,
The pump, the pile-driver, the great derrick, the coal-kiln and
    brickkiln,
Coal-mines and all that is down there, the lamps in the darkness,
    echoes, songs, what meditations, what vast native thoughts
    looking through smutch'd faces,
Iron-works, forge-fires in the mountains or by river-banks, men
    around feeling the melt with huge crowbars, lumps of ore, the
    due combining of ore, limestone, coal,
The blast-furnace and the puddling-furnace, the loup-lump at the
    bottom of the melt at last, the rolling-mill, the stumpy bars
    of pig-iron, the strong clean-shaped Trail for railroads,
Oil-works, silk-works, white-lead-works, the sugar-house,
    steam-saws, the great mills and factories,
Stone-cutting, shapely trimmings for facades or window or door-
    lintels, the mallet, the tooth-chisel, the jib to protect the
    thumb,

The calking-iron, the kettle of boiling vault-cement, and the fire
    under the kettle,
The cotton-bale, the stevedore's hook, the saw and buck of the
    sawyer, the mould of the moulder, the working-knife of the
    butcher, the ice-saw, and all the work with ice,
The work and tools of the rigger, grappler, sail-maker, block
    maker,
Goods of gutta-percha, papier-mache, colors, brushes, brush-
    making, glazier's implements,
The veneer and glue-pot, the confectioner's ornaments, the
    decanter and glasses, the shears and flat-iron,
The awl and knee-strap, the pint measure and quart measure, the
    counter and stool, the writing-pen of quill or metal, the
    making of all sorts of edged tools,
The brewery, brewing, the malt, the vats, every thing that is done
    by brewers, wine-makers, vinegar-makers,
Leather-dressing, coach-making, boiler-making, rope-twisting,
    distilling, sign-painting, lime-burning, cotton-picking,
    electroplating, electrotyping, stereotyping,
Stave-machines, planing-machines, reaping-machines,
    ploughing-machines, thrashing-machines, steam wagons,
The cart of the carman, the omnibus, the ponderous dray,
Pyrotechny, letting off color'd fireworks at night, fancy figures
    and jets;
Beef on the butcher's stall, the slaughter-house of the butcher,
    the butcher in his killing-clothes,
The pens of live pork, the killing-hammer, the hog-hook, the
    scalder's tub, gutting, the cutter's cleaver, the packer's maul,
    and the plenteous winterwork of pork-packing,
Flour-works, grinding of wheat, rye, maize, rice, the barrels and
    the half and quarter barrels, the loaded barges, the high piles
    on wharves and levees,
The men and the work of the men on ferries, railroads, coasters,
    fish-boats, canals;
The hourly routine of your own or any man's life, the shop, yard,
    store, or factory,

These shows all near you by day and night—workman! whoever
    you are, your daily life!

In that and them the heft of the heaviest—in that and them far
    more than you estimated, (and far less also,)
In them realities for you and me, in them poems for you and me,
In them, not yourself-you and your soul enclose all things,
    regardless of estimation,
In them the development good—in them all themes, hints,
    possibilities.

I do not affirm that what you see beyond is futile, I do not advise
    you to stop,
I do not say leadings you thought great are not great,
But I say that none lead to greater than these lead to.

Will you seek afar off? you surely come back at last,
In things best known to you finding the best, or as good as the
    best,
In folks nearest to you finding the sweetest, strongest, lovingest,
Happiness, knowledge, not in another place but this place, not
    for another hour but this hour,
Man in the first you see or touch, always in friend, brother,
    nighest neighbor—woman in mother, sister, wife,
The popular tastes and employments taking precedence in poems
    or anywhere,
You workwomen and workmen of these States having your own
    divine and strong life,
And all else giving place to men and women like you.
When the psalm sings instead of the singer,

When the script preaches instead of the preacher,
When the pulpit descends and goes instead of the carver that
    carved the supporting desk,
When I can touch the body of books by night or by day, and when

they touch my body back again,
When a university course convinces like a slumbering woman
and child convince,
When the minted gold in the vault smiles like the night
watchman's daughter,
When warrantee deeds loafe in chairs opposite and are my
friendly companions,
I intend to reach them my hand, and make as much of them as I
do of men and women like you.

To Think of Time

To think of time—of all that retrospection,
To think of to-day, and the ages continued henceforward.

Have you guess'd you yourself would not continue?
Have you dreaded these earth-beetles?
Have you fear'd the future would be nothing to you?

Is to-day nothing? is the beginningless past nothing?
If the future is nothing they are just as surely nothing.

To think that the sun rose in the east—that men and women were
    flexible, real, alive—that every thing was alive,
To think that you and I did not see, feel, think, nor bear our part,
To think that we are now here and bear our part.

Not a day passes, not a minute or second without an
    accouchement,
Not a day passes, not a minute or second without a corpse.

The dull nights go over and the dull days also,
The soreness of lying so much in bed goes over,
The physician after long putting off gives the silent and terrible
    look for an answer,
The children come hurried and weeping, and the brothers and
    sisters are sent for,
Medicines stand unused on the shelf, (the camphor-smell has
    long pervaded the rooms,)
The faithful hand of the living does not desert the hand of the
    dying,
The twitching lips press lightly on the forehead of the dying,
The breath ceases and the pulse of the heart ceases,

The corpse stretches on the bed and the living look upon it,
It is palpable as the living are palpable.

The living look upon the corpse with their eyesight,
But without eyesight lingers a different living and looks curiously
     on the corpse.

To think the thought of death merged in the thought of materials,
To think of all these wonders of city and country, and others
     taking great interest in them, and we taking no interest in
     them.

To think how eager we are in building our houses,
To think others shall be just as eager, and we quite indifferent.

(I see one building the house that serves him a few years, or
     seventy or eighty years at most,
I see one building the house that serves him longer than that.)

Slow-moving and black lines creep over the whole earth—they
     never cease—they are the burial lines,
He that was President was buried, and he that is now President
     shall surely be buried.

A reminiscence of the vulgar fate,
A frequent sample of the life and death of workmen,
Each after his kind.

Cold dash of waves at the ferry-wharf, posh and ice in the river,
     half-frozen mud in the streets,
A gray discouraged sky overhead, the short last daylight of
     December,
A hearse and stages, the funeral of an old Broadway stage-driver,

the cortege mostly drivers.

Steady the trot to the cemetery, duly rattles the death-bell,
The gate is pass'd, the new-dug grave is halted at, the living
     alight, the hearse uncloses,
The coffin is pass'd out, lower'd and settled, the whip is laid on
     the coffin, the earth is swiftly shovel'd in,
The mound above is flatted with the spades—silence,
A minute—no one moves or speaks—it is done,
He is decently put away—is there any thing more?

He was a good fellow, free-mouth'd, quick-temper'd, not bad
     looking,
Ready with life or death for a friend, fond of women, gambled,
     ate hearty, drank hearty,
Had known what it was to be flush, grew low-spirited toward the
     last, sicken'd, was help'd by a contribution,
Died, aged forty-one years—and that was his funeral.

Thumb extended, finger uplifted, apron, cape, gloves, strap,
     wet-weather clothes, whip carefully chosen,
Boss, spotter, starter, hostler, somebody loafing on you, you
     loafing on somebody, headway, man before and man behind,
Good day's work, bad day's work, pet stock, mean stock, first out,
     last out, turning-in at night,
To think that these are so much and so nigh to other drivers, and
     he there takes no interest in them.

The markets, the government, the working-man's wages, to think
     what account they are through our nights and days,
To think that other working-men will make just as great account
     of them, yet we make little or no account.

The vulgar and the refined, what you call sin and what you call
     goodness, to think how wide a difference,

85

To think the difference will still continue to others, yet we lie
    beyond the difference.

To think how much pleasure there is,
Do you enjoy yourself in the city? or engaged in business? or
    planning a nomination and election? or with your wife and
    family?
Or with your mother and sisters? or in womanly housework? or
    the beautiful maternal cares?
These also flow onward to others, you and I flow onward,
But in due time you and I shall take less interest in them.

Your farm, profits, crops—to think how engross'd you are,
To think there will still be farms, profits, crops, yet for you of
    what avail?

What will be will be well, for what is is well,
To take interest is well, and not to take interest shall be well.

The domestic joys, the dally housework or business, the building
    of houses, are not phantasms, they have weight, form,
    location,
Farms, profits, crops, markets, wages, government, are none of
    them phantasms,
The difference between sin and goodness is no delusion,
The earth is not an echo, man and his life and all the things of his
    life are well-consider'd.

You are not thrown to the winds, you gather certainly and safely
    around yourself,
Yourself! yourself!. yourself, for ever and ever!

It is not to diffuse you that you were born of your mother and
    father, it is to identify you,

It is not that you should be undecided, but that you should be
    decided,
Something long preparing and formless is arrived and form'd in
    you,
You are henceforth secure, whatever comes or goes.

The threads that were spun are gather'd, the wet crosses the
    warp, the pattern is systematic.

The preparations have every one been justified,
The orchestra have sufficiently tuned their instruments, the
    baton has given the signal.

The guest that was coming, he waited long, he is now housed,
He is one of those who are beautiful and happy, he is one of those
    that to look upon and be with is enough.

The law of the past cannot be eluded,
The law of the present and future cannot be eluded,
The law of the living cannot be eluded, it is eternal,
The law of promotion and transformation cannot be eluded,
The law of heroes and good-doers cannot be eluded,
The law of drunkards, informers, mean persons, not one iota
    thereof can be eluded.

Slow moving and black lines go ceaselessly over the earth,
Northerner goes carried and Southerner goes carried, and they
    on the Atlantic side and they on the Pacific,
And they between, and all through the Mississippi country, and
    all over the earth.

The great masters and kosmos are well as they go, the heroes and
    good-doers are well,
The known leaders and inventors and the rich owners and pious
    and distinguish'd may be well,

But there is more account than that, there is strict account of all.

The interminable hordes of the ignorant and wicked are not
    nothing,
The barbarians of Africa and Asia are not nothing,
The perpetual successions of shallow people are not nothing as
    they go.

Of and in all these things,
I have dream'd that we are not to be changed so much, nor the
    law of us changed,
I have dream'd that heroes and good-doers shall be under the
    present and past law,
And that murderers, drunkards, liars, shall be under the present
    and past law,
For I have dream'd that the law they are under now is enough.

And I have dream'd that the purpose and essence of the known
    life, the transient,
Is to form and decide identity for the unknown life, the
    permanent.

If all came but to ashes of dung,
If maggots and rats ended us, then Alarum! for we are betray'd,
Then indeed suspicion of death.

Do you suspect death? if I were to suspect death I should die now,
Do you think I could walk pleasantly and well-suited toward
    annihilation?

Pleasantly and well-suited I walk,
Whither I walk I cannot define, but I know it is good,
The whole universe indicates that it is good,
The past and the present indicate that it is good.

How beautiful and perfect are the animals!

How perfect the earth, and the minutest thing upon it!
What is called good is perfect, and what is called bad is just as
    perfect,
The vegetables and minerals are all perfect, and the
    imponderable fluids perfect;
Slowly and surely they have pass'd on to this, and slowly and
    surely they yet pass on.

I swear I think now that every thing without exception has an
    eternal soul!
The trees have, rooted in the ground! the weeds of the sea have!
    the animals!

I swear I think there is nothing but immortality!
That the exquisite scheme is for it, and the nebulous float is for
    it, and the cohering is for it!
And all preparation is for it—and identity is for it—and life and
    materials are altogether for it!

The Sleepers

I wander all night in my vision,
Stepping with light feet, swiftly and noiselessly stepping and
    stopping,
Bending with open eyes over the shut eyes of sleepers,
Wandering and confused, lost to myself, ill-assorted,
    contradictory,
Pausing, gazing, bending, and stopping.

How solemn they look there, stretch'd and still,
How quiet they breathe, the little children in their cradles.

The wretched features of ennuyes, the white features of corpses,
    the livid faces of drunkards, the sick-gray faces of onanists,
The gash'd bodies on battle-fields, the insane in their
    strong-door'd rooms, the sacred idiots, the new-born
    emerging from gates, and the dying emerging from gates,
The night pervades them and infolds them.

The married couple sleep calmly in their bed, he with his palm on
    the hip of the wife, and she with her palm on the hip of the
    husband,
The sisters sleep lovingly side by side in their bed,
The men sleep lovingly side by side in theirs,
And the mother sleeps with her little child carefully wrapt.

The blind sleep, and the deaf and dumb sleep,
The prisoner sleeps well in the prison, the runaway son sleeps,
The murderer that is to be hung next day, how does he sleep?
And the murder'd person, how does he sleep?

The female that loves unrequited sleeps,
And the male that loves unrequited sleeps,

The head of the money-maker that plotted all day sleeps,
And the enraged and treacherous dispositions, all, all sleep.

I stand in the dark with drooping eyes by the worst-suffering and
 the most restless,
I pass my hands soothingly to and fro a few inches from them,
The restless sink in their beds, they fitfully sleep.

Now I pierce the darkness, new beings appear,
The earth recedes from me into the night,
I saw that it was beautiful, and I see that what is not the earth is
 beautiful.

I go from bedside to bedside, I sleep close with the other sleepers
 each in turn,
I dream in my dream all the dreams of the other dreamers,
And I become the other dreamers.

I am a dance—play up there! the fit is whirling me fast!

I am the ever-laughing—it is new moon and twilight,
I see the hiding of douceurs, I see nimble ghosts whichever way
 look,
Cache and cache again deep in the ground and sea, and where it
 is neither ground nor sea.

Well do they do their jobs those journeymen divine,
Only from me can they hide nothing, and would not if they could,
I reckon I am their boss and they make me a pet besides,
And surround me and lead me and run ahead when I walk,
To lift their cunning covers to signify me with stretch'd arms, and
 resume the way;
Onward we move, a gay gang of blackguards! with mirth-
 shouting music and wild-flapping pennants of joy!

I am the actor, the actress, the voter, the politician,

The emigrant and the exile, the criminal that stood in the box,
He who has been famous and he who shall be famous after to
    day,
The stammerer, the well-form'd person, the wasted or feeble
    person.

I am she who adorn'd herself and folded her hair expectantly,
My truant lover has come, and it is dark.

Double yourself and receive me darkness,
Receive me and my lover too, he will not let me go without him.

I roll myself upon you as upon a bed, I resign myself to the dusk.

He whom I call answers me and takes the place of my lover,
He rises with me silently from the bed.

Darkness, you are gentler than my lover, his flesh was sweaty and
    panting,
I feel the hot moisture yet that he left me.

My hands are spread forth, I pass them in all directions,
I would sound up the shadowy shore to which you are journeying.

Be careful darkness! already what was it touch'd me?
I thought my lover had gone, else darkness and he are one,
I hear the heart-beat, I follow, I fade away.

I descend my western course, my sinews are flaccid,
Perfume and youth course through me and I am their wake.

It is my face yellow and wrinkled instead of the old woman's,
I sit low in a straw-bottom chair and carefully darn my
    grandson's stockings.

It is I too, the sleepless widow looking out on the winter
    midnight,
I see the sparkles of starshine on the icy and pallid earth.

A shroud I see and I am the shroud, I wrap a body and lie in the
    coffin,
It is dark here under ground, it is not evil or pain here, it is
    blank here, for reasons.

(It seems to me that every thing in the light and air ought to be
    happy,
Whoever is not in his coffin and the dark grave let him know he
    has enough.)

I see a beautiful gigantic swimmer swimming naked through the
    eddies of the sea,
His brown hair lies close and even to his head, he strikes out with
    courageous arms, he urges himself with his legs,
I see his white body, I see his undaunted eyes,
I hate the swift-running eddies that would dash him head-
    foremost on the rocks.

What are you doing you ruffianly red-trickled waves?
Will you kill the courageous giant? will you kill him in the prime
    of his middle age?

Steady and long he struggles,
He is baffled, bang'd, bruis'd, he holds out while his strength
    holds out,
The slapping eddies are spotted with his blood, they bear him
    away, they roll him, swing him, turn him,
His beautiful body is borne in the circling eddies, it is
    continually bruis'd on rocks,
Swiftly and ought of sight is borne the brave corpse.

I turn but do not extricate myself,
Confused, a past-reading, another, but with darkness yet.

The beach is cut by the razory ice-wind, the wreck-guns sound,
The tempest lulls, the moon comes floundering through the
    drifts.

I look where the ship helplessly heads end on, I hear the burst as
    she strikes, I hear the howls of dismay, they grow fainter and
    fainter.

I cannot aid with my wringing fingers,
I can but rush to the surf and let it drench me and freeze upon
    me.

I search with the crowd, not one of the company is wash'd to us
    alive,
In the morning I help pick up the dead and lay them in rows in a
    barn.

Now of the older war-days, the defeat at Brooklyn,
Washington stands inside the lines, he stands on the intrench'd
    hills amid a crowd of officers.
His face is cold and damp, he cannot repress the weeping drops,
He lifts the glass perpetually to his eyes, the color is blanch'd
    from his cheeks,
He sees the slaughter of the southern braves confided to him by
    their parents.

The same at last and at last when peace is declared,
He stands in the room of the old tavern, the well-belov'd soldiers
    all pass through,
The officers speechless and slow draw near in their turns,
The chief encircles their necks with his arm and kisses them on

the cheek,
He kisses lightly the wet cheeks one after another, he shakes
hands and bids good-by to the army.

Now what my mother told me one day as we sat at dinner
together,
Of when she was a nearly grown girl living home with her parents
on the old homestead.

A red squaw came one breakfast-time to the old homestead,
On her back she carried a bundle of rushes for rush-bottoming
chairs,
Her hair, straight, shiny, coarse, black, profuse, half-envelop'd
her face,
Her step was free and elastic, and her voice sounded exquisitely
as she spoke.

My mother look'd in delight and amazement at the stranger,
She look'd at the freshness of her tall-borne face and full and
pliant limbs,
The more she look'd upon her she loved her,
Never before had she seen such wonderful beauty and purity,
She made her sit on a bench by the jamb of the fireplace, she
cook'd food for her,
She had no work to give her, but she gave her remembrance and
fondness.

The red squaw staid all the forenoon, and toward the middle of
the afternoon she went away,
O my mother was loth to have her go away,
All the week she thought of her, she watch'd for her many a
month,
She remember'd her many a winter and many a summer,
But the red squaw never came nor was heard of there again.

A show of the summer softness—a contact of something unseen—
an amour of the light and air,
I am jealous and overwhelm'd with friendliness,
And will go gallivant with the light and air myself.

O love and summer, you are in the dreams and in me,
Autumn and winter are in the dreams, the farmer goes with his
thrift,
The droves and crops increase, the barns are well-fill'd.

Elements merge in the night, ships make tacks in the dreams,
The sailor sails, the exile returns home,
The fugitive returns unharm'd, the immigrant is back beyond
months and years,
The poor Irishman lives in the simple house of his childhood with
the well known neighbors and faces,
They warmly welcome him, he is barefoot again, he forgets he is
well off,
The Dutchman voyages home, and the Scotchman and
Welshman voyage
home, and the native of the Mediterranean voyages home,
To every port of England, France, Spain, enter well-fill'd ships,
The Swiss foots it toward his hills, the Prussian goes his way, the
Hungarian his way, and the Pole his way,
The Swede returns, and the Dane and Norwegian return.

The homeward bound and the outward bound,
The beautiful lost swimmer, the ennuye, the onanist, the female
that loves unrequited, the money-maker,
The actor and actress, those through with their parts and those
waiting to commence,
The affectionate boy, the husband and wife, the voter, the
nominee that is chosen and the nominee that has fail'd,
The great already known and the great any time after to-day,
The stammerer, the sick, the perfect-form'd, the homely,

The criminal that stood in the box, the judge that sat and
    sentenced him, the fluent lawyers, the jury, the audience,
The laugher and weeper, the dancer, the midnight widow, the red
    squaw,
The consumptive, the erysipalite, the idiot, he that is wrong'd,
The antipodes, and every one between this and them in the dark,
I swear they are averaged now—one is no better than the other,
The night and sleep have liken'd them and restored them.

I swear they are all beautiful,
Every one that sleeps is beautiful, every thing in the dim light is
    beautiful,
The wildest and bloodiest is over, and all is peace.

Peace is always beautiful,
The myth of heaven indicates peace and night.

The myth of heaven indicates the soul,
The soul is always beautiful, it appears more or it appears less, it
    comes or it lags behind,
It comes from its embower'd garden and looks pleasantly on itself
    and encloses the world,
Perfect and clean the genitals previously jetting,and perfect and
    clean the womb cohering,
The head well-grown proportion'd and plumb, and the bowels
    and joints proportion'd and plumb.

The soul is always beautiful,
The universe is duly in order, every thing is in its place,
What has arrived is in its place and what waits shall be in its
    place,
The twisted skull waits, the watery or rotten blood waits,
The child of the glutton or venerealee waits long, and the child of
    the drunkard waits long, and the drunkard himself waits long,
The sleepers that lived and died wait, the far advanced are to go
    on in their turns, and the far behind are to come on in their

turns,
The diverse shall be no less diverse, but they shall flow and
    unite — they unite now.

The sleepers are very beautiful as they lie unclothed,
They flow hand in hand over the whole earth from east to west as
    they lie unclothed,
The Asiatic and African are hand in hand, the European and
    American are hand in hand,
Learn'd and unlearn'd are hand in hand, and male and female are
    hand in hand,
The bare arm of the girl crosses the bare breast of her lover, they
    press close without lust, his lips press her neck,
The father holds his grown or ungrown son in his arms with
    measureless love, and the son holds the father in his arms
    with measureless love,
The white hair of the mother shines on the white wrist of the
    daughter,
The breath of the boy goes with the breath of the man, friend is
    inarm'd by friend,
The scholar kisses the teacher and the teacher kisses the scholar,
    the wrong'd made right,
The call of the slave is one with the master's call, and the master
    salutes the slave,
The felon steps forth from the prison, the insane becomes sane,
    the suffering of sick persons is reliev'd,
The sweatings and fevers stop, the throat that was unsound is
    sound, the lungs of the consumptive are resumed, the poor
    distress'd head is free,
The joints of the rheumatic move as smoothly as ever, and
    smoother than ever,
Stiflings and passages open, the paralyzed become supple,
The swell'd and convuls'd and congested awake to themselves in
    condition,
They pass the invigoration of the night and the chemistry of the

night, and awake.

I too pass from the night,
I stay a while away O night, but I return to you again and love
    you.

Why should I be afraid to trust myself to you?
I am not afraid, I have been well brought forward by you,
I love the rich running day, but I do not desert her in whom I lay
    so long,
I know not how I came of you and I know not where I go with you,
    but I know I came well and shall go well.

I will stop only a time with the night, and rise betimes,
I will duly pass the day O my mother, and duly return to you.

I Sing the Body Electric

I sing the body electric,
The armies of those I love engirth me and I engirth them,
They will not let me off till I go with them, respond to them,
And discorrupt them, and charge them full with the charge of the
    soul.

Was it doubted that those who corrupt their own bodies conceal
    themselves?
And if those who defile the living are as bad as they who defile the
    dead?
And if the body does not do fully as much as the soul?
And if the body were not the soul, what is the soul?

The love of the body of man or woman balks account, the body
    itself balks account,
That of the male is perfect, and that of the female is perfect.

The expression of the face balks account,
But the expression of a well-made man appears not only in his
    face,
It is in his limbs and joints also, it is curiously in the joints of
    his hips and wrists,
It is in his walk, the carriage of his neck, the flex of his waist
    and knees, dress does not hide him,
The strong sweet quality he has strikes through the cotton and
    broadcloth,
To see him pass conveys as much as the best poem, perhaps
    more,
You linger to see his back, and the back of his neck and
    shoulder-side.

The sprawl and fulness of babes, the bosoms and heads of
women, the folds of their dress, their style as we pass in the
street, the contour of their shape downwards,
The swimmer naked in the swimming-bath, seen as he swims
through the transparent green-shine, or lies with his face up
and rolls silently to and from the heave of the water,
The bending forward and backward of rowers in row-boats, the
horse-man in his saddle,
Girls, mothers, house-keepers, in all their performances,
The group of laborers seated at noon-time with their open
dinner-kettles, and their wives waiting,
The female soothing a child, the farmer's daughter in the garden
or cow-yard,
The young fellow hosing corn, the sleigh-driver driving his six
horses through the crowd,
The wrestle of wrestlers, two apprentice-boys, quite grown, lusty,
good-natured, native-born, out on the vacant lot at sundown
after work,
The coats and caps thrown down, the embrace of love and
resistance,
The upper-hold and under-hold, the hair rumpled over and
blinding the eyes;
The march of firemen in their own costumes, the play of
masculine muscle through clean-setting trowsers and waist
straps,
The slow return from the fire, the pause when the bell strikes
suddenly again, and the listening on the alert,
The natural, perfect, varied attitudes, the bent head, the curv'd
neck and the counting;
Such-like I love—I loosen myself, pass freely, am at the mother's
breast with the little child,
Swim with the swimmers, wrestle with wrestlers, march in line
with the firemen, and pause, listen, count.

I knew a man, a common farmer, the father of five sons,

And in them the fathers of sons, and in them the fathers of sons.

This man was a wonderful vigor, calmness, beauty of person,
The shape of his head, the pale yellow and white of his hair and
beard, the immeasurable meaning of his black eyes, the
richness and breadth of his manners,
These I used to go and visit him to see, he was wise also,
He was six feet tall, he was over eighty years old, his sons were
massive, clean, bearded, tan-faced, handsome,
They and his daughters loved him, all who saw him loved him,
They did not love him by allowance, they loved him with personal
love,
He drank water only, the blood show'd like scarlet through the
clear-brown skin of his face,
He was a frequent gunner and fisher, he sail'd his boat himself,
he had a fine one presented to him by a ship-joiner, he had
fowling-pieces presented to him by men that loved him,
When he went with his five sons and many grand-sons to hunt or
fish, you would pick him out as the most beautiful and
vigorous of the gang,
You would wish long and long to be with him, you would wish to
sit by him in the boat that you and he might touch each other.

I have perceiv'd that to be with those I like is enough,
To stop in company with the rest at evening is enough,
To be surrounded by beautiful, curious, breathing, laughing flesh
is enough,
To pass among them or touch any one, or rest my arm ever so
lightly round his or her neck for a moment, what is this then?
I do not ask any more delight, I swim in it as in a sea.

There is something in staying close to men and women and
looking on them, and in the contact and odor of them, that
pleases the soul well,
All things please the soul, but these please the soul well.

This is the female form,
A divine nimbus exhales from it from head to foot,
It attracts with fierce undeniable attraction,
I am drawn by its breath as if I were no more than a helpless
    vapor, all falls aside but myself and it,
Books, art, religion, time, the visible and solid earth, and what
    was expected of heaven or fear'd of hell, are now consumed,
Mad filaments, ungovernable shoots play out of it, the response
    likewise ungovernable,
Hair, bosom, hips, bend of legs, negligent falling hands all
    diffused, mine too diffused,
Ebb stung by the flow and flow stung by the ebb, love-flesh
    swelling and deliciously aching,
Limitless limpid jets of love hot and enormous, quivering jelly of
    love, white-blow and delirious nice,
Bridegroom night of love working surely and softly into the
    prostrate dawn,
Undulating into the willing and yielding day,
Lost in the cleave of the clasping and sweet-flesh'd day.

This the nucleus—after the child is born of woman, man is born
    of woman,
This the bath of birth, this the merge of small and large, and the
    outlet again.

Be not ashamed women, your privilege encloses the rest, and is
    the exit of the rest,
You are the gates of the body, and you are the gates of the soul.

The female contains all qualities and tempers them,
She is in her place and moves with perfect balance,
She is all things duly veil'd, she is both passive and active,
She is to conceive daughters as well as sons, and sons as well as
    daughters.

As I see my soul reflected in Nature,
As I see through a mist, One with inexpressible completeness,
    sanity, beauty,
See the bent head and arms folded over the breast, the Female I
    see.

The male is not less the soul nor more, he too is in his place,
He too is all qualities, he is action and power,
The flush of the known universe is in him,
Scorn becomes him well, and appetite and defiance become him
    well,
The wildest largest passions, bliss that is utmost, sorrow that is
    utmost become him well, pride is for him,
The full-spread pride of man is calming and excellent to the soul,
Knowledge becomes him, he likes it always, he brings every thing
    to the test of himself,
Whatever the survey, whatever the sea and the sail he strikes
    soundings at last only here,
(Where else does he strike soundings except here?)

The man's body is sacred and the woman's body is sacred,
No matter who it is, it is sacred—is it the meanest one in the
    laborers' gang?
Is it one of the dull-faced immigrants just landed on the wharf?
Each belongs here or anywhere just as much as the well-off, just
    as much as you,
Each has his or her place in the procession.

(All is a procession,
The universe is a procession with measured and perfect motion.)

Do you know so much yourself that you call the meanest
    ignorant?
Do you suppose you have a right to a good sight, and he or she

has no right to a sight?
Do you think matter has cohered together from its diffuse float,
    and the soil is on the surface, and water runs and vegetation
    sprouts,
For you only, and not for him and her?

A man's body at auction,
(For before the war I often go to the slave-mart and watch the
    sale,)
I help the auctioneer, the sloven does not half know his business.

Gentlemen look on this wonder,
Whatever the bids of the bidders they cannot be high enough for
    it,
For it the globe lay preparing quintillions of years without one
    animal or plant,
For it the revolving cycles truly and steadily roll'd.

In this head the all-baffling brain,
In it and below it the makings of heroes.

Examine these limbs, red, black, or white, they are cunning in
    tendon and nerve,
They shall be stript that you may see them.

Exquisite senses, life-lit eyes, pluck, volition,
Flakes of breast-muscle, pliant backbone and neck, flesh not
    flabby, good-sized arms and legs,
And wonders within there yet.

Within there runs blood,
The same old blood! the same red-running blood!
There swells and jets a heart, there all passions, desires,
    reachings, aspirations,
(Do you think they are not there because they are not express'd

106

in parlors and lecture-rooms?)

This is not only one man, this the father of those who shall be
    fathers in their turns,
In him the start of populous states and rich republics,
Of him countless immortal lives with countless embodiments
    and enjoyments.

How do you know who shall come from the offspring of his
    offspring through the centuries?
(Who might you find you have come from yourself, if you could
    trace back through the centuries?)

A woman's body at auction,
She too is not only herself, she is the teeming mother of mothers,
She is the bearer of them that shall grow and be mates to the
    mothers.

Have you ever loved the body of a woman?
Have you ever loved the body of a man?
Do you not see that these are exactly the same to all in all nations
    and times all over the earth?

If any thing is sacred the human body is sacred,
And the glory and sweet of a man is the token of manhood
    untainted,
And in man or woman a clean, strong, firm-fibred body, is more
    beautiful than the most beautiful face.

Have you seen the fool that corrupted his own live body? or the
    fool that corrupted her own live body?
For they do not conceal themselves, and cannot conceal
    themselves.

O my body! I dare not desert the likes of you in other men and
    women, nor the likes of the parts of you,
I believe the likes of you are to stand or fall with the likes of
    the soul, (and that they are the soul,)
I believe the likes of you shall stand or fall with my poems, and
    that they are my poems,
Man's, woman's, child, youth's, wife's, husband's, mother's,
    father's, young man's, young woman's poems,
Head, neck, hair, ears, drop and tympan of the ears,
Eyes, eye-fringes, iris of the eye, eyebrows, and the waking or
    sleeping of the lids,
Mouth, tongue, lips, teeth, roof of the mouth, jaws, and the jaw
    hinges,
Nose, nostrils of the nose, and the partition,
Cheeks, temples, forehead, chin, throat, back of the neck, neck
    slue,
Strong shoulders, manly beard, scapula, hind-shoulders, and the
    ample side-round of the chest,
Upper-arm, armpit, elbow-socket, lower-arm, arm-sinews, arm
    bones,
Wrist and wrist-joints, hand, palm, knuckles, thumb, forefinger,
    finger-joints, finger-nails,
Broad breast-front, curling hair of the breast, breast-bone,
    breast-side,
Ribs, belly, backbone, joints of the backbone,
Hips, hip-sockets, hip-strength, inward and outward round,
    man-balls, man-root,
Strong set of thighs, well carrying the trunk above,
Leg-fibres, knee, knee-pan, upper-leg, under-leg,
Ankles, instep, foot-ball, toes, toe-joints, the heel;
All attitudes, all the shapeliness, all the belongings of my or your
    body or of any one's body, male or female,
The lung-sponges, the stomach-sac, the bowels sweet and clean,
The brain in its folds inside the skull-frame,
Sympathies, heart-valves, palate-valves, sexuality, maternity,
Womanhood, and all that is a woman, and the man that comes

from woman,

The womb, the teats, nipples, breast-milk, tears, laughter,
weeping, love-looks, love-perturbations and risings,

The voice, articulation, language, whispering, shouting aloud,

Food, drink, pulse, digestion, sweat, sleep, walking, swimming,

Poise on the hips, leaping, reclining, embracing, arm-curving and
tightening,

The continual changes of the flex of the mouth, and around the
eyes,

The skin, the sunburnt shade, freckles, hair,

The curious sympathy one feels when feeling with the hand the
naked meat of the body,

The circling rivers the breath, and breathing it in and out,

The beauty of the waist, and thence of the hips, and thence
downward toward the knees,

The thin red jellies within you or within me, the bones and the
marrow in the bones,

The exquisite realization of health;

O I say these are not the parts and poems of the body only, but of
the soul,

O I say now these are the soul!

Faces

Sauntering the pavement or riding the country by-road, faces!
Faces of friendship, precision, caution, suavity, ideality,
The spiritual-prescient face, the always welcome common
    benevolent face,
The face of the singing of music, the grand faces of natural
    lawyers and judges broad at the back-top,
The faces of hunters and fishers bulged at the brows, the shaved
    blanch'd faces of orthodox citizens,
The pure, extravagant, yearning, questioning artist's face,
The ugly face of some beautiful soul, the handsome detested or
    despised face,
The sacred faces of infants, the illuminated face of the mother of
    many children,
The face of an amour, the face of veneration,
The face as of a dream, the face of an immobile rock,
The face withdrawn of its good and bad, a castrated face,
A wild hawk, his wings clipp'd by the clipper,
A stallion that yielded at last to the thongs and knife of the gelder.

Sauntering the pavement thus, or crossing the ceaseless ferry,
    faces and faces and faces,
I see them and complain not, and am content with all.

Do you suppose I could be content with all if I thought them their
    own finale?

This now is too lamentable a face for a man,
Some abject louse asking leave to be, cringing for it,
Some milk-nosed maggot blessing what lets it wrig to its hole.

This face is a dog's snout sniffing for garbage,

Snakes nest in that mouth, I hear the sibilant threat.

This face is a haze more chill than the arctic sea,
Its sleepy and wobbling icebergs crunch as they go.

This is a face of bitter herbs, this an emetic, they need no label,
And more of the drug-shelf, laudanum, caoutchouc, or hog's
    lard.

This face is an epilepsy, its wordless tongue gives out the
    unearthly cry,
Its veins down the neck distend, its eyes roll till they show
    nothing but their whites,
Its teeth grit, the palms of the hands are cut by the turn'd-in nails,
The man falls struggling and foaming to the ground, while he
    speculates well.

This face is bitten by vermin and worms,
And this is some murderer's knife with a half-pull'd scabbard.

This face owes to the sexton his dismalest fee,
An unceasing death-bell tolls there.

Features of my equals would you trick me with your creas'd and
    cadaverous march?
Well, you cannot trick me.

I see your rounded never-erased flow,
I see 'neath the rims of your haggard and mean disguises.

Splay and twist as you like, poke with the tangling fores of fishes
    or rats,
You'll be unmuzzled, you certainly will.

I saw the face of the most smear'd and slobbering idiot they had

111

at the asylum,
And I knew for my consolation what they knew not,
I knew of the agents that emptied and broke my brother,
The same wait to clear the rubbish from the fallen tenement,
And I shall look again in a score or two of ages,
And I shall meet the real landlord perfect and unharm'd, every
inch as good as myself.

The Lord advances, and yet advances,
Always the shadow in front, always the reach'd hand bringing up
the laggards.

Out of this face emerge banners and horses—O superb! I see what
is coming,
I see the high pioneer-caps, see staves of runners clearing the
way,
I hear victorious drums.

This face is a life-boat,
This is the face commanding and bearded, it asks no odds of the
rest,
This face is flavor'd fruit ready for eating,
This face of a healthy honest boy is the programme of all good.

These faces bear testimony slumbering or awake,
They show their descent from the Master himself.

Off the word I have spoken I except not one—red, white, black,
are all deific,
In each house is the ovum, it comes forth after a thousand years.

Spots or cracks at the windows do not disturb me,
Tall and sufficient stand behind and make signs to me,
I read the promise and patiently wait.

This is a full-grown lily's face,

She speaks to the limber-hipp'd man near the garden pickets,
Come here she blushingly cries, Come nigh to me limber-hipp'd
    man,
Stand at my side till I lean as high as I can upon you,
Fill me with albescent honey, bend down to me,
Rub to me with your chafing beard, rub to my breast and
    shoulders.

The old face of the mother of many children,
Whist! I am fully content.

Lull'd and late is the smoke of the First-day morning,
It hangs low over the rows of trees by the fences,
It hangs thin by the sassafras and wild-cherry and cat-brier under
    them.

I saw the rich ladies in full dress at the soiree,
I heard what the singers were singing so long,
Heard who sprang in crimson youth from the white froth and the
    water-blue.

Behold a woman!
She looks out from her quaker cap, her face is clearer and more
    beautiful than the sky.

She sits in an armchair under the shaded porch of the farmhouse,
The sun just shines on her old white head.

Her ample gown is of cream-hued linen,
Her grandsons raised the flax, and her grand-daughters spun it
    with the distaff and the wheel.

The melodious character of the earth,
The finish beyond which philosophy cannot go and does not wish
    to go,
The justified mother of men.

Song of the Answerer

Now list to my morning's romanza, I tell the signs of the
    Answerer,
To the cities and farms I sing as they spread in the sunshine
    before me.

A young man comes to me bearing a message from his brother,
How shall the young man know the whether and when of his
    brother?
Tell him to send me the signs. And I stand before the young man
    face to face, and take his right hand in my left hand and his
    left hand in my right hand,
And I answer for his brother and for men, and I answer for him
    that answers for all, and send these signs.

Him all wait for, him all yield up to, his word is decisive and final,
Him they accept, in him lave, in him perceive themselves as amid
    light,
Him they immerse and he immerses them.

Beautiful women, the haughtiest nations, laws, the landscape,
    people, animals,
The profound earth and its attributes and the unquiet ocean, (so
    tell I my morning's romanza,)
All enjoyments and properties and money, and whatever money
    will buy,
The best farms, others toiling and planting and he unavoidably
    reaps,
The noblest and costliest cities, others grading and building and
    he domiciles there,
Nothing for any one but what is for him, near and far are for him,
    the ships in the offing,
The perpetual shows and marches on land are for him if they are

for anybody.

He puts things in their attitudes,
He puts to-day out of himself with plasticity and love,
He places his own times, reminiscences, parents, brothers and
   sisters, associations, employment, politics, so that the rest
   never shame them afterward, nor assume to command them.

He is the Answerer,
What can be answer'd he answers, and what cannot be answer'd
   he shows how it cannot be answer'd.

A man is a summons and challenge,
(It is vain to skulk—do you hear that mocking and laughter? do
   you hear the ironical echoes?)

Books, friendships, philosophers, priests, action, pleasure, pride,
   beat up and down seeking to give satisfaction,
He indicates the satisfaction, and indicates them that beat up and
   down also.

Whichever the sex, whatever the season or place, he may go
   freshly and gently and safely by day or by night,
He has the pass-key of hearts, to him the response of the prying
   of hands on the knobs.

His welcome is universal, the flow of beauty is not more welcome
   or universal than he is,
The person he favors by day or sleeps with at night is blessed.

Every existence has its idiom, every thing has an idiom and
   tongue,
He resolves all tongues into his own and bestows it upon men,
   and any man translates, and any man translates himself also,
One part does not counteract another part, he is the joiner, he
   sees how they join.

He says indifferently and alike How are you friend? to the
    President at his levee,
And he says Good-day my brother, to Cudge that hoes in the
    sugar-field,
And both understand him and know that his speech is right.

He walks with perfect ease in the capitol,
He walks among the Congress, and one Representative says to
    another,
Here is our equal appearing and new.

Then the mechanics take him for a mechanic,
And the soldiers suppose him to be a soldier, and the sailors that
    he has follow'd the sea,
And the authors take him for an author, and the artists for an
    artist,
And the laborers perceive he could labor with them and love
    them,
No matter what the work is, that he is the one to follow it or has
    follow'd it,
No matter what the nation, that he might find his brothers and
    sisters there.

The English believe he comes of their English stock,
A Jew to the Jew he seems, a Russ to the Russ, usual and near,
    removed from none.

Whoever he looks at in the traveler's coffee-house claims him,
The Italian or Frenchman is sure, the German is sure, the
    Spaniard is sure, and the island Cuban is sure,
The engineer, the deck-hand on the great lakes, or on the
    Mississippi or St. Lawrence or Sacramento, or Hudson or
    Paumanok sound, claims him.

The gentleman of perfect blood acknowledges his perfect blood,

The insulter, the prostitute, the angry person, the beggar, see
    themselves in the ways of him, he strangely transmutes them,
They are not vile any more, they hardly know themselves they are
    so grown.

The indications and tally of time,
Perfect sanity shows the master among philosophs,
Time, always without break, indicates itself in parts,
What always indicates the poet is the crowd of the pleasant
    company of singers, and their words,
The words of the singers are the hours or minutes of the light or
    dark, but the words of the maker of poems are the general
    light and dark,
The maker of poems settles justice, reality, immortality,
His insight and power encircle things and the human race,
He is the glory and extract thus far of things and of the human
    race.

The singers do not beget, only the Poet begets,
The singers are welcom'd, understood, appear often enough, but
    rare has the day been, likewise the spot, of the birth of the
    maker of poems, the Answerer,
(Not every century nor every five centuries has contain'd such a
    day, for all its names.)

The singers of successive hours of centuries may have ostensible
    names, but the name of each of them is one of the singers,
The name of each is, eye-singer, ear-singer, head-singer,
    sweet-singer, night-singer, parlor-singer, love-singer,
    weird-singer, or something else.

All this time and at all times wait the words of true poems,
The words of true poems do not merely please,
The true poets are not followers of beauty but the august masters
    of beauty;

The greatness of sons is the exuding of the greatness of mothers
and fathers,
The words of true poems are the tuft and final applause of
science.

Divine instinct, breadth of vision, the law of reason, health,
rudeness of body, withdrawnness,
Gayety, sun-tan, air-sweetness, such are some of the words of
poems.

The sailor and traveler underlie the maker of poems, the
Answerer,
The builder, geometer, chemist, anatomist, phrenologist, artist,
all these underlie the maker of poems, the Answerer.

The words of the true poems give you more than poems,
They give you to form for yourself poems, religions, politics, war,
peace, behavior, histories, essays, daily life, and every thing
else,
They balance ranks, colors, races, creeds, and the sexes,
They do not seek beauty, they are sought,
Forever touching them or close upon them follows beauty,
longing, fain, love-sick.

They prepare for death, yet are they not the finish, but rather the
outset,
They bring none to his or her terminus or to be content and full,
Whom they take they take into space to behold the birth of stars,
to learn one of the meanings,
To launch off with absolute faith, to sweep through the ceaseless
rings and never be quiet again.

Europe [The 72d and 73d Years of These States]

Suddenly out of its stale and drowsy lair, the lair of slaves,
Like lightning it le'pt forth half startled at itself,
Its feet upon the ashes and the rags, its hands tight to the throats
of kings.

O hope and faith!
O aching close of exiled patriots' lives!
O many a sicken'd heart!
Turn back unto this day and make yourselves afresh.

And you, paid to defile the People—you liars, mark!
Not for numberless agonies, murders, lusts,
For court thieving in its manifold mean forms, worming from his
simplicity the poor man's wages,
For many a promise sworn by royal lips and broken and laugh'd
at in the breaking,

Then in their power not for all these did the blows strike revenge,
or the heads of the nobles fall;
The People scorn'd the ferocity of kings.

But the sweetness of mercy brew'd bitter destruction, and the
frighten'd monarchs come back,
Each comes in state with his train, hangman, priest, tax-gatherer,
Soldier, lawyer, lord, jailer, and sycophant.

Yet behind all lowering stealing, lo, a shape,
Vague as the night, draped interminably, head, front and form,
in scarlet folds,
Whose face and eyes none may see,

120

Out of its robes only this, the red robes lifted by the arm,
One finger crook'd pointed high over the top, like the head of a
    snake appears.

Meanwhile corpses lie in new-made graves, bloody corpses of
    young men,
The rope of the gibbet hangs heavily, the bullets of princes are
    flying, the creatures of power laugh aloud,
And all these things bear fruits, and they are good.

Those corpses of young men,
Those martyrs that hang from the gibbets, those hearts pierc'd by
    the gray lead,
Cold and motionless as they seem live elsewhere with
    unslaughter'd vitality.

They live in other young men O kings!
They live in brothers again ready to defy you,
They were purified by death, they were taught and exalted.

Not a grave of the murder'd for freedom but grows seed for
    freedom, in its turn to bear seed,
Which the winds carry afar and re-sow, and the rains and the
    snows nourish.

Not a disembodied spirit can the weapons of tyrants let loose,
But it stalks invisibly over the earth, whispering, counseling,
    cautioning.
Liberty, let others despair of you—I never despair of you.

Is the house shut? is the master away?
Nevertheless, be ready, be not weary of watching,
He will soon return, his messengers come anon.

A Boston [1854]

To get betimes in Boston town I rose this morning early,
Here's a good place at the corner, I must stand and see the show.

Clear the way there Jonathan!
Way for the President's marshal — way for the government
    cannon!
Way for the Federal foot and dragoons, (and the apparitions
    copiously tumbling.)

I love to look on the Stars and Stripes, I hope the fifes will play
    Yankee Doodle.
How bright shine the cutlasses of the foremost troops!
Every man holds his revolver, marching stiff through Boston
    town.

A fog follows, antiques of the same come limping,
Some appear wooden-legged, and some appear bandaged and
    bloodless.

Why this is indeed a show—it has called the dead out of the earth!
The old graveyards of the hills have hurried to see!
Phantoms! phantoms countless by flank and rear!
Cock'd hats of mothy mould—crutches made of mist!
Arms in slings—old men leaning on young men's shoulders.

What troubles you Yankee phantoms? what is all this chattering
    of bare gums?
Does the ague convulse your limbs? do you mistake your crutches
    for firelocks and level them?

If you blind your eyes with tears you will not see the President's
    marshal,

If you groan such groans you might balk the government cannon.

For shame old maniacs — bring down those toss'd arms, and let
    your white hair be,
Here gape your great grandsons, their wives gaze at them from
    the windows,
See how well dress'd, see how orderly they conduct themselves.

Worse and worse — can't you stand it? are you retreating?
Is this hour with the living too dead for you?

Retreat then — pell-mell!
To your graves — back — back to the hills old limpers!
I do not think you belong here anyhow.

But there is one thing that belongs here — shall I tell you what it
    is, gentlemen of Boston?

I will whisper it to the Mayor, he shall send a committee to
    England,
They shall get a grant from the Parliament, go with a cart to the
    royal vault,
Dig out King George's coffin, unwrap him quick from the
    graveclothes, box up his bones for a journey,
Find a swift Yankee clipper — here is freight for you, black-bellied
    clipper,
Up with your anchor — shake out your sails — steer straight
    toward Boston bay.

Now call for the President's marshal again, bring out the
    government cannon,
Fetch home the roarers from Congress, make another procession,
    guard it with foot and dragoons.

This centre-piece for them;
Look, all orderly citizens — look from the windows, women!

The committee open the box, set up the regal ribs, glue those that
     will not stay,
Clap the skull on top of the ribs, and clap a crown on top of the
     skull.
You have got your revenge, old buster — the crown is come to its
     own, and more than its own.

Stick your hands in your pockets, Jonathan — you are a made
     man from this day,
You are mighty cute — and here is one of your bargains.

There Was a Child Went Forth

There was a child went forth every day,
And the first object he look'd upon, that object he became,
And that object became part of him for the day or a certain part
    of the day,
Or for many years or stretching cycles of years.

The early lilacs became part of this child,
And grass and white and red morning-glories, and white and red
    clover, and the song of the phoebe-bird,
And the Third-month lambs and the sow's pink-faint litter, and
    the mare's foal and the cow's calf,
And the noisy brood of the barnyard or by the mire of the pond
    side,
And the fish suspending themselves so curiously below there, and
    the beautiful curious liquid,
And the water-plants with their graceful flat heads, all became
    part of him.

The field-sprouts of Fourth-month and Fifth-month became part
    of him,
Winter-grain sprouts and those of the light-yellow corn, and the
    esculent roots of the garden,
And the apple-trees cover'd with blossoms and the fruit
    afterward, and wood-berries, and the commonest weeds by
    the road,
And the old drunkard staggering home from the outhouse of the
    tavern whence he had lately risen,
And the schoolmistress that pass'd on her way to the school,
And the friendly boys that pass'd, and the quarrelsome boys,
And the tidy and fresh-cheek'd girls, and the barefoot negro boy
    and girl,
And all the changes of city and country wherever he went.

His own parents, he that had father'd him and she that had

conceiv'd him in her womb and birth'd him,
They gave this child more of themselves than that,
They gave him afterward every day, they became part of him.

The mother at home quietly placing the dishes on the supper
    table,
The mother with mild words, clean her cap and gown, a
    wholesome odor falling off her person and clothes as she
    walks by,
The father, strong, self-sufficient, manly, mean, anger'd, unjust,
The blow, the quick loud word, the tight bargain, the crafty lure,
The family usages, the language, the company, the furniture, the
    yearning and swelling heart,
Affection that will not be gainsay'd, the sense of what is real, the
    thought if after all it should prove unreal,
The doubts of day-time and the doubts of night-time, the curious
    whether and how,
Whether that which appears so is so, or is it all flashes and
    specks?
Men and women crowding fast in the streets, if they are not
    flashes and specks what are they?
The streets themselves and the facades of houses, and goods in
    the windows,
Vehicles, teams, the heavy-plank'd wharves, the huge crossing at
    the ferries,
The village on the highland seen from afar at sunset, the river
    between,
Shadows, aureola and mist, the light falling on roofs and gables
    of white or brown two miles off,
The schooner near by sleepily dropping down the tide, the little
    boat slack-tow'd astern,
The hurrying tumbling waves, quick-broken crests, slapping,
The strata of color'd clouds, the long bar of maroon-tint away
    solitary by itself, the spread of purity it lies motionless in,
The horizon's edge, the flying sea-crow, the fragrance of salt
    marsh and shore mud,
These became part of that child who went forth every day, and
    who now goes, and will always go forth every day.

Who Learns My Lesson Complete?

Who learns my lesson complete?
Boss, journeyman, apprentice, churchman and atheist,
The stupid and the wise thinker, parents and offspring,
    merchant, clerk, porter and customer,
Editor, author, artist, and schoolboy—draw nigh and commence;
It is no lesson—it lets down the bars to a good lesson,
And that to another, and every one to another still.

The great laws take and effuse without argument,
I am of the same style, for I am their friend,
I love them quits and quits, I do not halt and make salaams.

I lie abstracted and hear beautiful tales of things and the reasons
    of things,
They are so beautiful I nudge myself to listen.

I cannot say to any person what I hear—I cannot say it to myself—
    it is very wonderful.

It is no small matter, this round and delicious globe moving so
    exactly in its orbit for ever and ever, without one jolt or
    the untruth of a single second,
I do not think it was made in six days, nor in ten thousand years,
    nor ten billions of years,
Nor plann'd and built one thing after another as an architect
    plans and builds a house.

I do not think seventy years is the time of a man or woman,
Nor that seventy millions of years is the time of a man or woman,
Nor that years will ever stop the existence of me, or any one else.

Is it wonderful that I should be immortal? as every one is

immortal;
I know it is wonderful, but my eyesight is equally wonderful, and
    how I was conceived in my mother's womb is equally
    wonderful,
And pass'd from a babe in the creeping trance of a couple of
    summers and winters to articulate and walk—all this is
    equally wonderful.

And that my soul embraces you this hour, and we affect each
    other without ever seeing each other, and never perhaps to see
    each other, is every bit as wonderful.

And that I can think such thoughts as these is just as wonderful,
And that I can remind you, and you think them and know them
    to be true, is just as wonderful.

And that the moon spins round the earth and on with the earth,
    is equally wonderful,
And that they balance themselves with the sun and stars is
    equally wonderful.

Great Are The Myths

¹GREAT are the myths — I too delight in them;

Great are Adam and Eve — I too look back and accept them;

Great the risen and fallen nations and their poets, women, sages, inventors, rulers, warriors, and priests.

²Great is Liberty! great is Equality! I am their follower;

Helmsmen of nations, choose your craft! where you sail, I sail,

I weather it out with you, or sink with you.

³Great is Youth — equally great is Old Age — great are the Day and Night;

Great is Wealth — great is Poverty — great is Expression — great is Silence.

⁴Youth, large, lusty, loving — Youth, full of grace, force, fascination!

Do you know that Old Age may come after you, with equal grace, force, fascination?

⁵Day, full-blown and splendid — Day of the immense sun, action, ambition, laughter,

The Night follows close, with millions of suns, and sleep, and restoring darkness.

⁶Wealth, with the flush hand, fine clothes, hospitality;

But then the Soul's wealth, which is candor, knowledge, pride, enfolding love;

(Who goes for men and women showing Poverty richer than wealth?)

7Expression of speech! in what is written or said, forget not that Silence is also expressive,

That anguish as hot as the hottest, and contempt as cold as the coldest, may be without words.

8Great is the Earth, and the way it became what it is;

Do you imagine it has stopt at this? the increase abandon'd?

Understand then that it goes as far onward from this, as this is from the times when it lay in covering waters and gases, before man had appear'd.

9Great is the quality of Truth in man;

The quality of truth in man supports itself through all changes,

It is inevitably in the man — he and it are in love, and never leave each other.

10The truth in man is no dictum, it is vital as eyesight;

If there be any Soul, there is truth — if there be man or woman there is truth — if there be physical or moral, there is truth;

If there be equilibrium or volition, there is truth — if there be things at all upon the earth, there is truth.

[11]O truth of the earth! I am determin'd to press my way toward you;

Sound your voice! I scale mountains, or dive in the sea after you.

[12]Great is Language — it is the mightiest of the sciences,

It is the fulness, color, form, diversity of the earth, and of men and women, and of all qualities and processes;

It is greater than wealth — it is greater than buildings, ships, religions, paintings, music.

[13]Great is the English speech — what speech is so great as the English?

Great is the English brood — what brood has so vast a destiny as the English?

It is the mother of the brood that must rule the earth with the new rule;

The new rule shall rule as the Soul rules, and as the love, justice, equality in the Soul rule.

[14]Great is Law — great are the few old land-marks of the law,

They are the same in all times, and shall not be disturb'd.

[15]Great is Justice!

Justice is not settled by legislators and laws — it is in the Soul;

It cannot be varied by statutes, any more than love, pride, the attraction of gravity, can;

It is immutable — it does not depend on majorities — majorities or what not, come at last before the same passionless and exact tribunal.

[16]For justice are the grand natural lawyers, and perfect judges — is it in their Souls;

It is well assorted — they have not studied for nothing — the great includes the less;

They rule on the highest grounds—they oversee all eras, states, administrations.

[17]The perfect judge fears nothing — he could go front to front before God;

Before the perfect judge all shall stand back — life and death shall stand back—heaven and hell shall stand back.

[18]Great is Life, real and mystical, wherever and whoever;

Great is Death — sure as life holds all parts together, Death holds all parts together.

[19]Has Life much purport? — Ah, Death has the greatest purport.